CYLE

STARLIGHT HIGHLANDER MAIL ORDER BRIDES 3

SKYE MACKINNON

Peryton Press

CONTENTS

GLOSSARY

Many of the alien words are taken from Scottish Gaelic (yes, including the flying vagina). Some of them have been slightly changed, while others are exact translations.

Albya – planet of the Albyans (from Alba = Scotland)

Bainnse – wedding

Bawbag – scrotum (Scots insult)

Click – minute (30 Earth minutes are 20 intergalactic clicks)

C-suit – camouflage suit that helps aliens blend in with humans

Fraoch – a shrub plant similar to heather

Hogmanay – the Scottish New Year's Eve

Lady Beyra – Albyan Goddess (based on the Scottish/Celtic Beira myth)

Leannan – sweetheart, my love

Migges – midges (tiny mosquitos aka miniature demons who love to torment this particular author in her garden)

Pit air iteig – for fuck's sake (literally: flying vagina)

Rotation – Albyan year

Quantnet – intergalactic internet

Sgid/sgidding – fuck/fucking

Taigeis – a fluffy round animal based on the Scottish haggis

Ton air eigh dhut – fuck you (literally: may your arse hit the ice)

Uisge beatha – whisky (literally: water of life)

1

Cyle

For the first time in a rotational decade, I felt a spark of hope that this wasn't the end of my species. Seeing my brother with his new mate fed my drive to find a solution. They were mates even though she was an alien. Nobody had thought it possible, yet here they were, handfasted and utterly in love.

Ever since returning from Peritus, or Earth, as the natives called their planet, I'd spent all my waking hours in my lab. After sleeping on my chair for several nights, a bed magically appeared in my office. On one of my many to-do lists was a note to increase my assistant's rise. He always knew what I needed before I did. Without him, I'd probably forget to eat and sleep altogether.

The weight of responsibility weighed heavily on my shoulders. I was Albya's First Scientist, and it was therefore my task to find a solution to our extinction problem. There were two strands to the issue: finding new female mates on other planets and curing the Sleep that had affected our own females. For almost a generation, our females had been comatose. No cause or cure had ever been found. Many had perished since, but there were still enough left to restart our population.

Some people preferred finding a cure. They didn't want to mix our species with another.

They didn't know what I knew. My father had burdened me with the terrible secret before he'd killed himself out of guilt, taking my mother with him. Not even my brother knew. I was the only Albyan who was aware of what had really happened. How the Sleep had swept over our females.

Yet even that knowledge hadn't helped me in finding a cure. I'd spent all my adult life trying to find a solution. If I didn't find one, we'd go extinct. Already, males outnumbered females twenty-to-one. Some of the females slumbering in their deep Sleep were no longer fertile. And even before the Sleep, fertility rates had gone down.

That's why a few years ago, I'd shifted the priority of my research to finding mates among the stars. I'd sent out probes, traded genetic samples with other species, travelled to all the space stations in the galactic region. All in the hope of discovering a species compatible with Albyans.

And then I'd found them. Peritans. A primitive species on a backwater planet that had only just begun taking its first steps into space. If the Intergalactic University hadn't provided me with copious samples to replicate my results, I would have discarded them as an option. I'd been looking for species that had travelled the stars for aeons, who may have had contact with Albyans and carried part of our genetic code.

After seeing just how similar Peritans were to us – although they lacked mating antennae and a second set of arms – I'd come up with various theories. I couldn't prove it, but I was convinced that Albyans may have landed on their planet long ago, adding to their gene pool, making the mating bond possible.

I looked at the image of my brother and his mate that I had flung onto the screen opposite my desk. It was for motivation. The way they looked at each other with adoration, the way Thorrn held her in his arms, it was all I needed to put all my energy into my research. One day, I might find a mate myself. But not until I had found a cure. I'd sworn that to myself at the very beginning. And I never broke a promise. Never.

My commstick beeped, reminding me that it was time to head to the spaceport. The first batch of alien females was about to arrive. The Peritan dating agency

I cooperated with had sent me the genetic code of about a hundred of their candidates. It had been a moment of true joy when I'd discovered ten clear matches. There were more potential matches, but I didn't have enough data yet to verify those connections. Once the ten females arrived and met their males, I'd be able to study them. The males had all agreed to various tests. I couldn't wait for the data to come in. After not a single positive result in years, this was almost overwhelming.

I'd calculated that we'd need at least 250 breeding couples to keep our species alive. If all ten matches worked as well as that of Thorrn and Jenny, that left only 239 to go. The unsurmountable task that had loomed over me for so long now seemed almost achievable. Of course, I wanted more than just 250 males to find their mates. If only such a small number of Albyans got a female, there was a danger of jealousy, violence, even civil war. The Council of Elders had warned me about publicising the magic number, so I'd kept it to myself.

The commstick vibrated again, but I stayed seated. Something made me want to stay here. As a scientist, I felt the need to analyse my emotions and motivations. I was a logical person. I rarely got emotional. But now, some strange feeling made my stomach clench. I closed my eyes and examined my emotions before they got too overwhelming.

Worry. Sadness. Anticipation. Fear.

I delved further into my heart, separating the individual feelings to analyse them. It was an exercise I'd done since my childhood. My mother had taught me. Sometimes, my emotions had taken control and I'd acted without thinking. This was my strategy to prevent that from happening.

I was worried that not all ten matches would happen.

I was sad that I wasn't one of the males at the spaceport waiting for their Peritan female to arrive.

I was excited that this was finally happening. That a solution may be in sight.

And I was scared that I would never get a mate. That I'd stay alone forever. That I'd have to watch my brother and his mate be happy together, have offspring, have the kind of life every Albyan dreamed about.

This last emotion worried me. This fear could easily lead to jealousy. Both would distract me from my work. I had to stay cool-headed and use pure logic to fulfil my mission.

I breathed in deep, held my breath for a click until I could no longer, then breathed out, pushing all those unruly feelings out of my mind.

When I opened my eyes again, I was calm. And I knew that going to the spaceport wasn't a good idea. It was better if I stayed in my lab and worked on determining the next batch of potential mates. Now that all Albyans knew of Thorrn and Jenny, they were eager to get their own female. I hadn't thought the pressure on me to succeed could get any greater, but I'd been wrong. An entire planet was putting its faith in my team and me.

I couldn't fail.

If I did, Albya would cease to exist.

Vhom, my assistant, didn't seem surprised in the slightest to find me hunched over the holobase, swirling DNA fragments around like puzzle pieces. I'd found three more matches already. The algorithms were starting to learn and I no longer had to do as much manual searching. In maybe another ten matches, they should be extensive enough to do this on their own.

"Three matches!" Vhom exclaimed, leaning over the holobase. "That's excellent. Anyone we know?"

I shrugged. "I didn't look at the names, just their database number. Names don't matter."

Vhom tsked. "Maybe not for you, but for the three males you just found a mate for, it will matter more than all the stars in the universe. May I look?"

I knew he secretly hoped that one of those males was him. It was a microscopically small chance, but I decided to indulge him.

"Go ahead. Why aren't you at the greeting ceremony at the spaceport? I assumed everyone would go."

My assistant sighed. "I don't think I could stand it. I'm not a jealous male, but..."

"I understand," I admitted, surprising myself. "Would you like to watch it from here?"

"I'd rather not. Is there anything I can help you with instead?"

I mentally went through the list of tasks that I'd paid no attention to since we'd returned from Peritus. I'd been too elated to think of all the things I did routinely.

"You could check on our control group of sleeping females," I suggested. "I've not done that in a while. I doubt anything has changed, but we need to keep adding to our data."

Vhom nodded. "I will."

I remembered that one of the females we'd been observing since the beginning of the Sleep was his mother. Vhom was still young; he'd been a boy when the Sleep had come, so it was no surprise she was still alive. As long as Vhom's father lived, she'd survive for many more rotational decades.

It was one of the strange things about the Sleep that females died when their mates perished. They simply stopped breathing as if they were somehow bound to the fate of their males. Females who'd been mated to other females stayed alive, both of them trapped in the Sleep.

My assistant left the lab and I focused on my task once more, finding matches among Peritans and Albyans, all the while wishing that one of those females was meant for me.

2

Beth

After a month spent on a spaceship, it felt good to have solid ground beneath my feet once again. After the first few days, I'd no longer noticed the slight vibrations, but now that we stood on a planet – a freaking alien planet! – I realised just how much I'd got used to the movement. My legs tingled, although that may have been due to the different gravity. Or the atmosphere.

Everything here was new. And that was exactly what I wanted.

"Laura, you're matched to Khran."

I watched as one of the younger women, a punk with bright blue hair and a temper to match, stepped away from our group and towards the human woman who was organising the welcome ceremony. She'd introduced herself as Jenny and told us she'd been matched to an Albyan male before she'd even realised that he was an alien.

By now, I was used to their appearance. In fact, I couldn't imagine them without their second pair of arms, their bare chests, their kilts and dainty antennae. I'd used my four-week stay on the Starlight to learn as much about them as possible. The captain, Ghorr, had taken me under his wing after learning that I was an engineer and showed me the workings of the ship. I knew he'd hoped his mating antennae would activate to prove that I was his mate, but they never did. I liked him as a friend, nothing more. Just before I'd disembarked, Ghorr had invited me to stay at his estate in the foothills of the Daor Mountains. He'd made it sound like paradise on Earth - well, Albya - so I was definitely going to take him up on that offer at some point. But first, it was time to meet my mate.

"Beth, you're matched to Obi."

I knew that. I'd looked at his photograph every day since I'd been given his sparse file. Obi. A giant of a man. About forty years old in Earth time. An architect who specialised in building offices. Silver rings around his antennae stalks. A stubbly beard. And not a smile in sight. Not on the picture and not now that he stepped away from the other males.

Maybe he had a physical problem that prevented him from smiling. I grabbed my handbag a little tighter and walked towards him.

Khran had tried to hug Laura. Obi didn't do such a thing. Maybe he didn't want to touch me. My scars tended to have that effect on people. They either turned away in revulsion or treated me as if their touch could break me. Or ignored me as if I wasn't even there.

Obi looked at me with bright green eyes – the same colour as his kilt – and held out all four of his hands. I had to suppress a grin. He looked ridiculous. I shook his lower two. His grip was weak as if he didn't want to hurt me. His lips finally curved into a semblance of a smile, but it looked forced.

"Welcome to Albya," he said, his small smile already disappearing.

His voice did nothing for me. I was all about voices. I'd listened to more audiobooks than I could count during our voyage across the stars. My phone was stuffed full of podcasts and yet more audiobooks. Deep, velvety male voices made me melt. Obi did not have such a voice.

I looked him up and down and felt nothing.

A slight commotion made me swirl around to see my friend June being kissed by her mate. He had all four arms wrapped around her and it didn't look like he had any intention of letting her go. And she was kissing him back. I grinned. June had been one of the more sceptical women who wouldn't have boarded the Starlight if she'd known just where it was headed. I, on the other hand, had been delighted to find out that we were travelling to an alien planet. The further away from my old life, the better.

"Do you want me to kiss you?" Obi asked. He didn't sound as if he wanted to.

"No," I said and realised it was the first word I'd spoken to him. This wasn't going like I'd planned. For the past month, I'd imagined what our first meeting would be like. The Albyan crew had told us that we'd feel the mating bond right away. For both Laura and Khran, and June and her alien, it looked like it had been an instant attraction. People didn't just kiss the first time they met without a certain pull towards each other.

I felt no such pull. Obi was no different than any of the other males in the room.

Maybe the mating bond needed physical touch to be triggered. Our handshake may not have been enough.

"Alright, kiss me," I said.

In my dreams, Obi had wrapped his arms around me to pull me close before kissing me passionately. In reality, he simply leaned down and pressed his lips on mine. And didn't move more than that. This had to be the most awkward kiss in the history of Albya. He simply stood there as if he didn't know what to do next. Had he never kissed before?

I cupped his face and opened my lips, hoping he'd get the hint.

He stayed frozen. No reaction at all.

I wanted to cry. This wasn't at all what I'd imagined. The Beth of the past, before the accident, would have cried. But I didn't. I'd not cried since my husband's funeral. The last two years had made me a hard woman, erasing all softness and vulnerability. My heart was locked inside a steel bunker. I'd hoped that my Albyan mate might find a key to it. Now, I suspected it might never be released from the chains I'd wrapped around it.

I stepped away from the male I was matched to. He licked his lips, then also took a step back, putting even more space between us.

We stood there awkwardly. I didn't know what to do. I didn't want to do small talk with my mate. We'd been told our connection would be instant. We'd feel like we'd known each other forever. Like childhood friends, finally reunited.

I felt nothing.

"Your attention, please!" Jenny called out. I was glad for the distraction. It gave me a reason to turn away from Obi. "We've prepared some nibbles for you all, so you can stay here for as long as you want. Ladies, you can decide whether you want to stay in a hotel in town or accompany your match to their home. No pressure. We want you to feel comfortable. Albyans, please give your females as much space as they need. If they prefer to sleep in a hotel, don't make them feel bad about it. I know you're all very keen to get to know your mates, but trust me, this will take time."

I let my gaze wander across the room. Most males looked disappointed at Jenny's words. It would be interesting to see who would go with their alien and who would stay at a hotel. I definitely knew what I was going to do.

I turned back to Obi. He wasn't looking at me. Yes, I most certainly wasn't going to stay with him tonight. We needed more time to get to know each other.

Watching the other couples made me realise how different Obi and I were. The other pairs all stood close to each other, leaning into their mate's personal space seemingly without being aware of it. You could almost see the pull between them. Some had given up resisting it and openly held hands already. None were as passionate as June and her mate, though. I looked for them, but they'd left the room. I smirked, imagining what they might be up to. I had no doubts that they'd end up in bed by tomorrow at the latest.

"Shall we leave?" Obi asked me. "I have a shuttle parked nearby."

"Leave? Go to your home, you mean?"

"Of course. Why stay here? We can talk at home. Say your goodbyes."

He still didn't smile. And he expected me to go to his house without even having any kind of connection? No way.

"I'm going to stay at a hotel," I said firmly. "We can meet up tomorrow."

He frowned. I was almost glad to see that his expression could change and wasn't always passive. "But you're my mate. You should stay with me."

"Right now, we're not mates. We were matched by the agency. If I understand correctly, we only become mates once we've done the handfasting ceremony, right?"

"Or until the male claims his female," he said in his monotonous voice. "I intend to claim you tonight."

I took a step back. What the fuck was he talking about? Was he in some other reality where we already knew each other, loved each other? There was no way on Earth - or Albya - I was going to jump into bed with him. I'd not had sex since my husband had passed away. The next time I let a man touch me, it had to be meaningful and precious. No one-night-stands for me.

"No, I'm going to a hotel."

I turned away, but he grabbed my arm and swirled me around until I was facing him again.

"You're my female," he said with a soft growl. "You're going to stay with me. It will look bad if you don't."

Look bad. I almost laughed. He was concerned about appearances. I supposed Albya wasn't all that different from Earth.

"I don't care what people think," I hissed, now properly angry. "Look at my face. I've learned to ignore their stares, their whispered comments. I'm not going to your house just because you're worried about what others will say. Tomorrow, we can meet and start over. For now, I'm going to bed."

I extracted myself from his grip and hurried off. I wanted to talk to Jenny, but I couldn't see her anywhere. The other women were all busy talking to their matches - or kissing them, in at least two cases. A sour feeling was settling in my stomach. I was jealous of how easy they took to their aliens. The thought of kissing Obi made me want to puke. Maybe it would change once I'd actually had a chance to get to know him. He was a stranger. And an arse.

"Can I help you?" an Albyan male asked. It took me a moment to recognise him as one of the guys from the Starlight. He now wore a black-and-gold kilt like all the other waiters and helpers.

"Yes, thanks. I'd like to go to the hotel now."

He looked over my shoulder. "You're matched to Obi?"

"Aye. How did you know?"

"Because he's glaring at me as if he wants to rip off my antennae." He chuckled. I wished I could remember his name. He'd not been one of the Albyans who'd spent a lot of time with us. I was almost sure I'd once seen him covered in a flour-like substance in the kitchen.

"He can glare as much as he likes," I said, trying to be more confident than I felt. "I need my own space tonight."

"Understandably. I can't even imagine how it must feel to be on a different planet, surrounded by people you don't know. I'll organise a shuttle for you. Your belongings will be brought to the hotel. They might even get there before you."

He pulled out his commstick. At the touch of a button, a holographic square appeared above it. I'd come to learn that most Albyans had configured their commstick to suit their way of thinking. Some used numbers and letters, others shapes, others colours. I liked how the technology adapted depending on how its user's brain worked best.

"I'll take you to the shuttle," he said after a moment. I had no idea how manipulating some shapes had ordered a taxi, but so be it. Captain Ghorr had said that we'd be given our own commsticks once we'd arrived so we could communicate with each other and with people on Earth.

"Let go of my female!" Obi's shout came a fraction of a second before I was pushed from behind. I stumbled, tripped, and ended up on all fours on the floor. A glass shattered next to me, exploding into tiny shards. Above me, grunts and the sound of fists hitting flesh weaved a fabric of noise that clung to me, pushing me away from reality and into the abyss of my memories.

People shouting. Groans of exhaustion and pain. Squeaking metal. Whispering flames. The smell of acrid smoke. The cuts of a thousand shards. And above it all, Kade's screams.

I curled into a ball. Back then, I'd been trapped, unable to move, unable to protect myself. Now, I made myself as small as possible, waiting for it all to be over. I pressed my hands against my ears, shutting out all sound. With my eyes squeezed shut, I could imagine I was in another place, another time.

We'd gone caving once. A birthday present. I'd thought I'd be scared in the dark, damp cave, but I'd loved every minute of it. Standing in the darkness, up to my hips in cold water, I'd felt connected to the depths of the Earth. It had been a raw, primal experience. The memory had become my refuge later, whenever everything got too much. I imagined myself in the cave, surrounded by solid earth that had been there since the beginning of time. It was a safe place where I could be alone without feeling lonely.

I stayed in my mental cave until the noise stopped. I slowly opened my eyes. Jenny kneeled by my side. The Albyans had left, with a few of them forming a protective ring around us but keeping their distance. There was no sign of Obi.

"Are you alright?" Jenny asked, then tsked. "Of course, you aren't. Let's get you to a hotel and then we'll talk in the morning. Your match totally misbehaved. My mate will have a chat with him."

She helped me to my feet and led me to a shuttle. I stayed quiet throughout the flight, just going through the motions. I didn't want to think about my situation.

But when I lay in bed, a soft blanket moulding around my body, I couldn't ignore the facts any longer.

I was on a different planet.

I was matched to an alien I had no feelings for.

A male I was starting to hate.

3

Cyle

My commstick's irritating ringtone woke me. It took me a moment to realise where I was. Not my home. I'd slept at the lab again. This was becoming a bad habit again. The trip to Peritus had ripped me out of my routine and I thought that finding compatible females would be enough to stop me from overworking myself.

I'd been wrong.

The commstick vibrated again. Sgidding thing. I sighed and answered the call without looking at the holo display.

"Yes?"

"You sound awful, brother." It was Thorrn. My idiot brother who'd somehow managed to get a mate before anyone else.

"Why are you calling me this early?"

Thorrn chuckled. "It's not early. You've slept in. And you might want to look at the video I sent. You missed a whole lot of fun at the welcome ceremony last night."

"Fun?" I repeated while slowly sitting up. My mouth was dry. When had I last drunk or eaten something? I couldn't remember when I'd stopped working. I'd been so busy finding new matches, over thirty of them. It had been exhilarating. I'd completely forgotten about the ceremony.

"Eron and his mate gave quite the show. You'll want to watch it, trust me."

Intriguing. I staggered over to my desk and pulled up my messages. Thorrn wasn't the only one who'd sent me the video. It seemed it had gone viral. I threw it onto the biggest screen and watched as Eron snatched up his mate and kissed her passionately. I was getting ready to send him a very pointed message when I realised that the female was kissing him back. She was just as affected as he was.

The video jumped to a second scene. Eron's female - I dimly remembered her name to be June - was talking to another male I didn't recognise. He reached out to her and suddenly, Eron barged in, pushing him so hard the other male fell to the floor, before wrapping the female in his arms. Again, she didn't seem to mind. How very curious. I hadn't expected such a strong reaction at the first meeting. Eron and June had instantly catapulted themselves to the top of my list. I was planning to run tests on all the ten matches, but this was so extraordinary that I'd happily ignore them all for now. It was a definite advantage that Eron was a childhood friend.

If I hadn't known him since we could barely walk, I'd have thought him entirely unsuited for having a female. He was a recluse, a hermit, and the grumpiest male on the planet. But he hadn't always been this way. Once, he'd been the life and soul of any party. He had more friends than I'd ever hope to find. But not long after the Sleep, he'd changed and moved out of the capital and into the middle of nowhere.

I pulled up an image of his mate. June. If their first encounter was anything to go by, she'd do him good. I might get my friend back.

Not that I had time for friends.

I pulled some nutrient bars from a cupboard – not the tastiest of foods but the most convenient – and started going over the data. At first glance, the genetic markers determining that Eron and June were mates looked no different from that of the other matches. I would have never suspected them of behaving differently. There had to be something else.

I barely noticed Vhom coming in. He sat a cup of tea on my table, but when I remembered to thank him, he was already gone. I took a long sip and closed my eyes for a moment. I'd not had enough sleep, but the tea should help with that. It was yoipy tea, made from the leaves of a rare plant, and my favourite. I should give Vhom a pay rise.

The yoipy plant had a unique structure. Male and female plants grew wrapped around each other, forming a column as high as a tall Albyan. When they reached maturity, their tips fused together, creating a permanent bond. From the fused tip, flower pods sprouted, containing fertilised seeds that were carried away by insects. A lone yoipy plant didn't survive. There always had to be two of them. And they didn't become fertile until they fused together.

I opened my eyes and stared at the data in front of me. Maybe...

If my theory proved correct, Vhom would get promoted.

I rummaged for my communicator.

"Want to prod me again?" Jenny asked without a greeting. I knew she was joking, but I did feel bad for stealing her away from Thorrn so often. It felt like she'd spent more time at my lab than at home with her mate.

"No, not today. We're taking a trip to a taigeis farm."

The shuttle landed gently on soft ground. Eron still hadn't created a proper landing area for shuttles, so we'd had to set down on a field.

"This is exciting," Jenny cheered. "I've not been out of Priomh before."

"Keep your distance from the taigeis. They're vicious." I hopped out first before assisting her. Peritan legs were so short and Thorrn would kill me if his mate twisted her ankle.

The smell of animal excrement made me sneeze. And this was why I didn't come here more often. Dirt was everywhere. The sound of hundreds of taigeis chittering was almost as bad as the stink.

Eron and June greeted us and from the moment I saw them, I could feel their connection. They probably weren't aware of how they moved in the same way, kept seeking each other's touch. They gravitated towards each other like yoipy plants. Once they'd finished becoming one unit, they'd be fertile. Offspring. The first Albyan children to be born in a generation.

Inside, away from the smell of the animals, I scanned them from top to toe. They indulged me, letting me take all the readings I needed while Jenny chatted with June.

"Good, I think I've got the basics," I announced and pulled out my latest invention, a scanner more sensitive than any I'd used before. "Now kiss."

Eron's mouth gaped open as he stared at me. "You want us to kiss now? In front of you?"

I had a hard time keeping a straight face. "You didn't have any problem with that at the spaceport."

He looked like he was about to punch me. His mate, however, pulled him close and cupped his cheeks with her small hands. "Let's give them the show of their lives," she whispered before pressing her lips to his.

My heart ached as I watched them kiss passionately. What would it feel like to have a female in my arms? Would her lips be as soft as I imagined? Would she give herself to me like June with Eron?

I almost forgot to turn on the scanner. Forcing myself to concentrate on the readings, I watched as data ran over the screen. It was too early to tell, but I had a good feeling about it. The data matched my theory, but I'd have to examine it in detail in my lab.

Before I could stop myself, I looked at them, still kissing, but now running their hands over each other. "Good," I said quickly before they went any further. "This is very good."

"Pervert," Jenny muttered under her breath. "Get your own mate."

Her words hurt. Didn't she know that I'd do anything to have a mate? After seeing her and Thorrn, June and Eron, I craved nothing more. But I couldn't, not yet. Even if I found my mate tomorrow, I'd have to wait. I made a promise and I wouldn't break it.

Jenny's communicator beeped and she answered a call. She spoke in hushed tones before turning to me. "We have to get back. One of the women has run away from her match. She sent me a message earlier today saying that she wasn't happy with him, but I didn't think she'd do anything this drastic."

"Who?" June asked before I could.

"Beth," Jenny said. "I'll have to go. Cyle, can you do your tests another time?"

I nodded and packed up my equipment as fast as possible.

Beth. I remembered matching her to a male called Obi. I didn't know him, but that was going to change as soon as we got back. Despite all the scenarios I'd considered, a female running away from her male hadn't crossed my mind. I'd have to find her and make sure she was safe. If anything happened to her, it would be my fault. I'd matched them.

What if I'd made a mistake? What if they weren't mates?

As soon as I'd set the shuttle to autopilot, I searched for the footage of last night's welcoming ceremony. I couldn't remember what Obi looked like, but Beth's image popped up in my head immediately. She'd been the only female who'd not looked Albyan. Instead of bright red hair and pale skin like the others – like all the other females and every Albyan on the planet – she had beautiful dark skin that had intrigued me from the start. Until our visit to Peritus, I hadn't realised that not all of their species looked like us. It made for a fascinating diversity that we didn't have on Albya.

"I should have gone to her this morning," Jenny muttered. "Their first meeting yesterday was awful. She ended up having a panic attack. I told her to stay at the hotel, but..."

"It's not your fault," I told her without taking my eyes off the footage. With all the matches, you could see their attraction right away. The males' antennae twitched and leaned forward as soon as they spotted their mates. The females seemed to gravitate towards their matches, staying close to them throughout the evening.

But not Beth. I zoomed into their first encounter, paying particular attention to Obi. His antennae didn't move. He rubbed them several times as if he expected a reaction, but from the way the two of them stood apart, it was evident that they didn't feel the same pull as the other couples.

I cursed myself for not going to the ceremony. I could have spotted this. It was clear to see for anyone who knew what they were looking for.

When he kissed her, a growl broke from my throat.

"Ew, that's disgusting," Jenny said, echoing my thoughts. "It's like they're in kindergarten trying their first kiss."

I didn't know what she was talking about and I wasn't sure I wanted to. Albyans only kissed their mates. Nobody else. After the Sleep, some of us sought relief in the arms of another male, but unless they were same-sex mates, they didn't kiss. I never did that. I was too busy searching for a cure.

I watched in horror as Obi pursued Beth, pushed her to the ground before attacking the male Beth had been talking to. While she was on the floor, curled into a ball, unmoving, other Albyans restrained Obi. The look on his face made a shiver run down my back.

"Are you sure she ran away?" I asked Jenny when a terrible thought struck my mind. "Or could he have taken her against her will?"

4

The Daor mountains reached up high, tickling the clouds. Snow covered their ragged peaks, glittering in the afternoon sun. A flock of bright blue birds were shadowing our shuttle, cawing so loudly that we could hear it even through the thick walls.

"Almost there," Ghorr announced and pointed to one of the smaller mountains to our right. "My estate is at the foot of Dun Beag. I'm glad it's such a beautiful day. You get to appreciate the Daor mountains in all their glory."

He smiled at me. He probably wasn't aware that he was rubbing his right antenna again. He'd been doing it throughout the flight. I half-wished his antennae would activate, signalling that I was his mate. But just like with Obi, I didn't feel anything for him. Not romantically, anyway. I liked Ghorr a lot, and I wanted him to be my friend. I was grateful he'd come to my hotel with the offer of taking me away for a few days. I'd not hesitated. Not after Obi's visit in the morning.

He'd come to my room while I'd still been asleep. I'd planned to meet him in a public place, over breakfast maybe, but instead, he hammered on my door, demanding to be let in. I didn't open. I was scared that he might make good on his words from last night, taking me as his mate.

But I wasn't his mate. I knew that in my heart. And I had enough self-respect left to refuse to be in a relationship with him. Genetics be damned. So what if we'd been matched in some lab by some scientist. We didn't match in real life. He was a bully who thought I belonged to him.

He'd stayed outside my room for at least an hour, shouting, banging against the door, until hotel personnel had escorted him outside. After I'd figured out how to use the communication system, I'd managed to call Jenny. She'd promised she'd deal with Obi, but I'd not heard back from her for hours.

And then Ghorr came and invited me to stay with him. There had been no question of what to do. This was my chance of getting away from Obi, see something of the planet and spend time with someone who actually wanted my company for who I was, not who I was supposed to be.

The flight had taken several hours and it was now late afternoon. I no longer wore a watch and had no commstick to check the time, but if the sun moved its way across the sky in the same way as our sun on Earth, it had to be at least 4pm. We'd learned on board the Starlight that Albyan days were slightly longer, but not dramatically so. It shouldn't take long to get used to it.

If I stayed.

When I'd discovered that we were going to a different planet, that we were going to meet aliens – and not just meet them, be their mates – I'd been ecstatic. Most of the other women on the Starlight had been angry or scared, but I'd seen it for what it was: the chance of a new life. A new beginning.

I'd dreamed of settling down with my alien mate. Starting afresh. Leaving my old life, my memories, my pain behind.

Now, I wasn't so sure anymore. Maybe returning to Earth would be best. We had to stay for a month, that's what the contract stipulated, but after that, we were free to choose whether we wanted to remain on Albya or leave.

The shuttle slowly descended and I finally got a view of Ghorr's estate. He was right in calling it that. Four buildings hugged the mountain's flank, with the largest looking as if it continued *inside* the mountain. Colourful fields were sprawled around it. Vegetables?

Flowers? I didn't know enough about Albyan flora to tell.

"That building to the right is a distillery," Ghorr said proudly. "My father's father set it up when he was my age. It's now one of the most successful uisge beatha distilleries in Albya."

That would explain the size of his estate. I hadn't realised how wealthy Ghorr was. He probably earned good money as a spaceship's captain, but he clearly came from money.

"Who else lives here?" I asked.

"The house next to the distillery is home to seven permanent staff. Then there's my brother, but like me, he has his own ship and rarely spends time here. My mother and two sisters are asleep and I have three assistants to look after them and the house. They keep me updated and run the day-to-day business. I have an uncle who sometimes comes to stay at the main house, but he's become frail and prefers to stay in the city where he's closer to medical facilities."

"What about your father?"

I regretted asking the question when I saw his expression change from proud to something darker. "He's not here. We don't talk about him."

Okay then. Curious. And not my business.

"I had the assistants prepare a room for you as well as some food," Ghorr said, now smiling again. "You must be hungry."

I was. My last meal had breakfast at the hotel, delivered to my door after I'd refused to go to the main restaurant in fear that Obi might turn up there. Half of the dishes had been inedible – or maybe I'd simply not known how to eat them – and I'd been too nervous to do more than nibble on the others.

Ghorr did one more circle above the estate before gently setting us down on a circular space that reminded me of a heliport, just bigger. Ghorr's shuttle was larger than the one I'd taken to the hotel. We'd been sitting in the cockpit together, but he'd shown me the main cabin when we'd boarded and there'd been space for at least ten people. More of a small bus than a car.

Did everyone on Albya have their own shuttle? Did everyone fly or did they have ground transportation? I couldn't remember them ever talking about this in our lessons back on the Starlight. Or maybe I'd missed that one while I was hanging out with Ghorr.

Two Albyans hurried towards the shuttle, both wearing the same kilt as the Captain, a crimson-and-black tartan. That meant they were of the same clan. We'd been taught that Albyan society was split into clans rather than countries. Each clan sent representatives to the Council of Elders in Priomh, where decisions that affected the entire planet were made. Many clans had their own languages but thanks to BrainTrain technology, everyone also spoke Albyan Prime. It was the same way we'd been taught the planet's common language during the flight: earplugs worn at night that made us learn a new language without even realising.

"Is everything alright?" Ghorr asked. He'd already got up and was waiting for me to follow him out of the cockpit.

I forced myself to focus and smiled at my knight in crimson kilt. "Everything's fine, sorry. I'm just a bit tired."

"Understandably. It's been two stressful days for you. I'll let you retire shortly, but first, you need to eat something. Follow me."

The air outside was cool and it smelled like rain was coming. The scent of flowers I didn't recognise reached my nose and I breathed in deep. I'd not spent enough time outdoors. Being locked up on the Starlight for a month had made me truly appreciate nature and even just the simply joy of breathing fresh air.

"The scent of beatha flowers always make me feel at home," Ghorr said with a smile. "The flowers are used in the distillery to give the uisge beatha a little extra flavour. It's why ours is the best."

One of the males got my suitcases from the shuttle while another greeted us by touching his forehead with his upper right fist. I did the same, glad I finally got to use what I'd learned on the Starlight. The male's eyes widened a little before a wide grin spread on his face.

"I hadn't realised that you'd found a mate, laird," he said to Ghorr. "She's most precious."

"*She*," I shot back, "is nobody's mate. I'm Ghorr's guest."

The Albyan took a step back and I almost felt sorry for how embarrassed he looked. But I didn't like it when people jumped to conclusions before they had all the information. As an engineer, making decisions without having all the data could be devastating.

"Beth is correct, Han," Ghorr weighed in. "She's here as my guest for as long as she likes. Please make sure she has everything she needs. I'm going to give her a tour of the distillery tomorrow and if the weather's nice, you can ready the sledge so we can explore the mountains."

"Sledge?" I asked. "Like in a wooden sledge that you use in the snow?"

Ghorr frowned in confusion. "No, that must be a translation error. A sledge is a small craft that can both drive on land and fly at low heights. It's perfect for short but arduous distances."

"Can't wait to see it."

He gave me a knowing look. "And you'll want to know exactly how it works."

"Of course." I grinned. "But right now, I'd like to be introduced to your food. I'm starving."

Our conversation over dinner made me once again wish that Ghorr was my mate. He was intelligent, kind, curious and even had a good sense of humour. Not quite as wicked as my own, but it was enough to make him a potential partner. But no matter how often he rubbed his antennae, there was no spark between us.

Han gave me intrigued looks while he served the food, but otherwise stayed in the background, only appearing when my glass or plate were empty. I'd not seen the other Albyan male again who'd dealt with my baggage. Ghorr had mentioned a third assistant, but I'd not seen him yet. It was strange to not have any women around. Everything was done by men. Tall, muscular, slightly intimidating men.

It was crazy to think that right now, there were only eleven women on this planet who were *awake*.

"Will you introduce me to your mother and sisters?" I asked after putting down my dessert spork. I'd come to love the Albyan eating utensils on the Starlight and was never going back to what we'd used on Earth.

Ghorr looked at me with confusion. "They're sleeping. They won't respond."

"I know. But..."

Now I had to explain. I shouldn't have said anything.

"I was in an accident," I said quietly. "They put me into an induced coma because I had swelling on the brain. The strange thing is, I remember some things from while I was unconscious. Conversations by my bedside. Nurses washing my body. Smells and sounds. Songs that played on the radio. Most of them are fragments, but I know that I was aware of my surroundings at least sometimes. I'm grateful that the nurses and doctors all treated me like I was awake, telling me what they were doing. There was one night nurse who'd read to me. I... Anyway, maybe it's the same for your females who're trapped in the Sleep, so I thought it would be nice to give them some new stimulation. Someone new."

Ghorr's expression softened and his eyes glistened. Was he getting teary?

"You're very kind," he whispered. "I'll introduce you to them tomorrow. For now-"

An irritating beep interrupted him. He pulled out his commstick and his face fell when he looked at the holoscreen.

"Uh oh. I think we're in trouble."

5

Obi was furious.

I was even angrier.

I wanted to punch the male before cutting off his dick and feeding it to Eron's taigeis. My brother Thorrn was the fighter, not me. I'd never been particularly aggressive, but right now, I was at the very edge of restraint. One more snide word from him about Beth would tip me over the edge.

"Find my mate!" Obi roared. "She needs to be with me."

The hotel guests around us gave us curious looks, but I forced myself to ignore them. They probably recognised me. My face had been all over the news after we'd announced that we'd found alien females compatible with us. As the First Scientist of Albya, I'd had to step out of the shadows and into the media's bright lights. I hated every moment I had to spend giving interviews instead of doing research in my lab.

"What do you think we're trying to do?" I hissed. "Every enforcer in Priomh is looking for her. Jenny is going over the hotel's security footage as we speak. And my brother is talking to the hotel staff. One of whom already told me about the scene you caused this morning. What were you thinking?"

Mother Beyra, help me. I wanted to punch him so bad. Obi had come to the hotel and shouted at poor Beth for at least an hour. Luckily, she'd not let him into her room. I didn't want to imagine what could have happened if she had. This male was deranged, dangerous. He didn't deserve a female. Especially not Beth.

"She's mine," he growled. "She was assigned to me. She belongs to me."

I couldn't hold back any longer. I grabbed him by the shoulders and pushed him against the wall as hard as I could.

"She doesn't belong to you," I spat. "You don't deserve her. And she wasn't *assigned* to you. She was matched, by me, based on your genetic markers. Clearly, I made a mistake."

He froze and for a moment, I hoped that he saw reason, but then fury sparked in his eyes and he retaliated. He slammed two hands against my chest, making me stagger back. I managed to catch my balance and avoid one of his fists before it could crash into my jaw, but I was too slow to evade his other. Pain erupted in my stomach.

If he wanted a fight, he could have it. I'd sparred with my brother often enough to know how to defend myself. He'd caught me unawares, but now I was ready for him. And furious.

I caught one of his fists just before the impact, my palm stinging, and twisted his wrist backwards. Dirty but effective. He yowled in agony and tried to punch me again, but his aim was off and I easily deflected him. I managed to get in two punches of my own, relishing the squeaks of pain he made.

He should be glad that I was too angry to focus on my knowledge of the Albyan body. If I wanted to, I could cause him unimaginable pain by pressing some choice spots that most people didn't even know about. I could kill him with a well-placed strike. But right now, I needed the mindless motion of my fists slamming into him, the pain whenever he slipped past my defences.

Sweat dripped down my back. I'd not had a physical workout in ages and I regretted that now. Luckily, Obi wasn't any fitter than me. He was an office worker and it showed. He was breathing hard and his punches were slowing. It was time to end the fight.

"Ton air eigh dhut[1]," I snarled before swiping his legs out from under him. He went down in a heap and didn't get up again.

I stumbled backwards, my pain only really registering now. I was a mess. I'd lost count of how often Obi had punched me. My chest was going to be littered in bruises soon if I didn't get to a medpod. I didn't even want to know what my face looked like.

I wiped across my mouth and my hand came back bloody. Pit air itaig. At least he'd not gone for my antennae. No honourable Albyan did that, but I wouldn't have put it past Obi.

A hotel employee hastened towards me and handed me a cloth. "We have a medpod on the second floor," he said with a sympathetic smile. He shot a glare towards Obi and lowered his voice. "He deserved it. The way he treated the female was repugnant. I tried to intervene, but he punched me. When I returned with backup, he'd left."

"He punched you?" I repeated and smiled. "Without provocation?"

The male nodded.

"Perfect. Finally, some good news." I pulled out my commstick and sent a quick message to the enforcers' bureau. Sometimes, being the First Scientist had its advantages. I had contacts in all the right places.

I smiled at the employee. "He's going to be arrested for that. Our... altercation was mutual, but with you, it was unprovoked. This means we're rid of him for a bit and can focus on what's important. Finding Beth."

I wiped my face and chest with the cloth, getting most of the blood and sweat off me. The pain was just about bearable, but I was looking forward to the medpod. But not until I'd found Beth. I wouldn't waste time by spending twenty IG clicks in a medpod when I could be searching for her instead.

Three enforcers strode into the lobby and I wordlessly pointed at Obi, still on the floor. He made a pitiful sight. They dragged him off. Someone started to applaud in the background.

"Cyle!" my brother shouted from behind me. "We – what the sgidding sgid have you done?"

"A little argument with Obi."

His eyebrows shot up in appreciation. "I knew there was a fighter somewhere within you, brother. That gash on your temple might even turn into a scar if you let it. We shall celebrate with a dram tonight. But first, I know who's taken Beth."

My heart skipped a beat. "She's been taken?"

He nodded grimly. "Ghorr. The Starlight's Captain. One of the hotel attendants recognised him and Jenny found the corresponding footage. He left the hotel with Beth. Her bags are gone. There are no signs of struggle, but we have to remember how much bigger we are compared to the Peritan females. Even a male such as Obi could coerce her by physical strength alone, and Ghorr is larger than this piece of sgid."

This time, I opened a voice channel to the enforcers' bureau rather than send a message.

"One of the Peritan females has been taken by Ghorr of Clan Iasg, Captain of the Starlight. She may be held against her will."

I looked at my brother, my throat dry. He put two hands on my shoulders and squeezed reassuringly.

"They'll get her back," he promised, and I believed him.

My hands were shaking. I kept looking at the screen to my right with the irrational fear that I might have missed a call. The bureau's chief had given me an update not long ago, but that had only heightened my anxiety. They'd established that Ghorr had taken Beth to his estate in the Daor mountains. Local enforcers were on their way to retrieve her with force, if necessary.

I would have stepped on the next shuttle if my rational mind hadn't told me that it would take hours to get to Ghorr's estate and that it made more sense to let the enforcers deal with it.

Instead, I'd returned to my lab to look at Beth and Obi's data. I'd clearly made a mistake when I'd matched the two, but how? Where? If their match was invalid, what did that mean for the programme? We were relying on a Peritan dating agency, Hot Tatties, to supply us with the genetic data of potential mates. If they discovered that I'd made a mistake, they might cancel their side of the agreement. It had taken forever to get the Intergalactic Council's permission to even transport Peritans off their planet. If the IGC decided to remove that permission... The Albyan race would be doomed. Ten females weren't enough to keep our species alive.

I shook my head, forcing myself to focus on the holobase in front of me. In the background, the AI was already recalculating every scrap of data I had on both Beth and Obi, but I also wanted to go over it manually. Sometimes, a machine didn't recognise the instinctual connections an Albyan could see.

But no matter how often I looked at the part of their genomes that signified the match, I always came to the same conclusion. They were mates. It made me want to throw up. They were most definitely not mates. Couldn't be. I was missing something.

In a fit of desperation, I connected my scanners to the database and transferred all the readings I'd done on Eron and June. Right now, I didn't care about the mystery of why the two of them had reacted to each other as they had, but who knew, it could help.

"You should go to a medpod before you get a permanent scar," Vhom said. I'd not even noticed him entering the lab. As always, my assistant was right. The gash above my left eyebrow had stopped bleeding, but it was wide enough to scar. Very few Albyans had scars. Some of them, like my brother, got them on purpose by refusing to step into a medpod. He always said it made him look more intimidating, which helped when facing opponents in the ring. I, however, was a scientist who spent most of his life in the lab. If I ever found a mate of my own, I didn't want her to think me ugly because of a scar.

Beth's image floated into my mind and I revised my opinion. Her face was scarred, yet she was beautiful. The scars only made her more beautiful, highlighting her strength and resilience.

"What's that?" Vhom asked and pointed at the holobase.

"It's the markers that-" I gasped as I realised the data had changed. Instead of one main marker on their genome, the display now highlighted two. Impossible. I would have noticed that before. But... would I? Had I looked for it? No. The marker I'd used to establish matches was the same that all Albyan carried. It caused Albyan males and females to be mates. Humans had the same sequence, so I'd assumed we matched in the same way. But here it was, a secondary marker.

I quickly scrolled through the data until I found Thorrn's and Jenny's genome. My heart was racing by the time I found the second highlighted marker. They both had it.

I pulled up a random Albyan mate-pair. Only the male had the secondary marker, not the female.

"That's astonishing," Vhom muttered. "Only Peritan females have that matching sequence. How can that be?"

"I don't know. But look, ten of the eleven Peritan-Albyan matches have it. Except for one. Beth and Obi don't match there. They're not mates."

The relief I felt was incredible. It didn't matter that I'd overlooked this. Beth wasn't tied to that male. And that meant... maybe she had a different mate.

I took a deep breath and restarted the matching algorithm, changing the parameters to take the secondary marker into account. It took the AI only a fraction of a click, but it felt as long as a rotation. Two images floated above the holobase. Beth and a male. Her mate.

Vhom gasped, then started laughing.

I didn't know how to react. What to think. Laughing hysterically seemed like a good idea. Or fainting.

This had to be a dream. This wasn't real.

I ran the algorithm again. And again.

I got the same result every single time.

Beth was my mate.

———————————

1. Ton air eigh dhut – fuck you (literally: may your arse hit the ice)

6

Beth

When I'd agreed to accompany Ghorr to his home, I'd expected peace and quiet. Time away from Obi. Some more interesting conversations with the Starlight's captain. The chance to explore Albya, my new home.

Instead, I got twenty men in black body suits crashing into the room, weapons drawn, shouting for us to get on the floor. I was too stunned to even react. When I finally got the clarity to move, someone had already wrapped their arms around me and I was pulled from the room faster than I could see.

Before I knew what was happening, I was outside, surrounded by three massive Albyans.

"Are you hurt? Did he hurt you?"

One of them, a giant with strange metal caps over his antennae – probably for protection – held out a device and pointed it at me.

"No injuries detected," he reported.

The tension lessened visibly. The guy next to him touched his forehead with his fist in greeting and I did the same.

"I'm Lovhu, head of the local enforcer bureau," he introduced himself. "We were told that you've been taken by Captain Ghorr. Everyone will be pleased that you're unhurt."

"Everyone?" I repeated weakly. I was still processing what was going on. Taken? Did they think I'd been kidnapped?

"The First Scientist personally oversaw the mission. The Council of Elders got involved also. If anything had happened to you, it would have affected all of Albya."

I gulped. What a mess. I'd never thought how this was a bit of a political issue. Time to fess up.

"I went out of my own free will. Ghorr didn't take me by force. He simply offered me a place to stay for a while. I accepted his offer. I'm sorry, I didn't think Obi would call the police. The enforcers, I mean."

"He didn't call us," Lovhu said before turning to one of his men who were pooling out of the building. "False alarm. Get back to the shuttle."

"He didn't?"

"If I'm informed correctly, the hotel got in touch with the Peritan female Jenny, who then informed her mate and the First Scientist. Now that we've established that you're well, I'll contact them with an update. Please wait here until I have new orders on what to do."

"I suppose staying here is out of the question?"

Lovhu gave me a sympathetic smile. "I think it is."

He talked into his commstick, but something weird happened and I didn't hear a single word of what he was saying. It was as if an invisible soundproof bubble had appeared around him. Handy. Although it left me curious.

What a day. My arrival on Albya really hadn't gone the way I'd hoped. I looked up at the mountain peaks, now black shadows against a purple sky. The sun had already set and soon, it would be completely dark. I was tired, but I doubted I'd get to sleep anytime soon.

"I'm to take you back to Priomh," Lovhu said and pocketed his commstick.

"To Obi?" I asked, dread rising in me. If he said yes, I'd run.

"No. I've been told to take you right to the First Scientist. He has some things to discuss with you."

Probably to tell me that I was Obi's mate and should stay with him. Well, that scientist was going to find out soon enough that I couldn't be ordered around. I wasn't going to be with Obi. No way. I'd rather sleep on the streets until the Starlight could take me back to Earth.

I fell asleep on the shuttle and only woke when someone gently touched my arm. The police shuttle had a bed – probably meant for casualties – and I'd made full use of it. The Albyan males had kept their distance and with Lovhu in the cockpit, sleeping had been the best thing to do.

I opened my eyes to see Jenny, with her mate Thorrn closely behind her.

"You alright?" she asked.

"Why does everyone keep asking me that? I'm fine. I was fine with Ghorr. The only person I wasn't fine with was Obi."

She sighed. "I know. I'm sorry about that. It turns out there's been a mistake, but Cyle wants to tell you himself. I can stay if you want me to, though."

"Cyle is the scientist, right?"

Thorrn leant over his mate and nodded. "The First Scientist of Albya. And my brother. You'll be safe with him. He's an honourable male. He kicked the sgid out of Obi for you earlier. He might even have a scar."

"Wait, he assaulted Obi? And got hurt? But I don't even know him."

Jenny chuckled. "You will soon enough. Follow me. Thorrn, get out of the way, you big blob of muscle."

Instead of stepping back, Thorrn wrapped his lower set of arms around Jenny's waist and lifted her into his arms. With a satisfied grin, he carried her out of the shuttle, ignoring her squeals.

I sat up, still a little groggy. I wasn't sure what had happened to my bags, if they were still at Ghorr's place or on this shuttle. I didn't even have a handbag since I had neither Albyan money nor a commstick as a replacement for my phone. Not that it mattered. I was starting to feel like a ball being passed around. I hated it. Hated feeling out of control.

I gritted my teeth and decided to listen to whatever that Cyle guy had to say and then find somewhere to stay. Pam at Hot Tatties had said that we'd get a stipend, so maybe I could find out how to access that money and pay for a hotel room myself.

When I stepped outside, an Albyan held an umbrella-like shield over my head. It was raining. The air was thick with moisture and I greedily breathed it in. I loved rain. I wanted to rip off my clothes and dance in it. Wash off all memories of Obi.

"This way," the male said and led me to a tall glass tower. Albyans really loved glass. Or whatever material it was that looked like glass. Rain ran down its sides like tears.

Jenny waited inside, no longer in Thorrn's arms. He stood behind her, looking sheepish like he'd just been told off by his mother. Jenny had her hands full with that one.

"Thorrn, want to make us a hot drink? I'll take Beth to Cyle's lab."

Lab? Were they going to run tests? Try to prove that I was Obi's mate?

"I'd rather go to the hotel again," I said and crossed my arms in front of my chest. "I'm not a lab rat."

To my surprise, Jenny laughed. "That's what I tell Cyle every time I'm here. One time, he looked up rats on the quantnet and then formally agreed with me that I was not a rat. It was hilarious. Sometimes, these guys just take everything too literally. But don't worry, you're not here to be tested and prodded. He just wants to talk. One thing you need to know about Cyle: he almost never leaves his lab. And if he's not in the laboratory, he's in his office. He's a complete workaholic. So meeting him here is normal. He'd probably go on dates in his lab, if he had a mate."

Relieved, I followed her. Thorrn disappeared at some point, presumably to make us a drink. I could do with a hot chocolate. It was cold inside the building. The corridors were empty, unsurprising since it was the middle of the night.

"Thanks for being here," I told Jenny. "I know it's late."

"Don't mention it. To be honest, I'm curious what Cyle discovered. He refused to tell me. Not even Thorrn knows."

That made me even more worried. If it was a secret, it had to be bad.

We stopped outside a glass door that had a strange milky fog swirling within, turning it opaque.

Jenny knocked. What a mundane, human thing to do. After everything that had happened today, this simple gesture felt out of place. Did Albyans knock?

When nobody answered, Jenny shrugged and strode into the room. I followed her, having to force my legs to walk. Every fibre in me was telling me to run.

The scientist sat on the edge of a glass table, both sets of arms crossed over his chest. The wall behind him was made up of dozens of screens. Most of them showed lines of numbers and letters that made no sense to me, but in the centre was a picture of me next to one of Obi. A shudder ran down my back. I should leave. Right now.

Cyle looked just like his brother. They had the same nose, the same eyes. Although Thorn had his shoulder-length hair braided and Cyle wore his loose. His expression was a confusing mix of contemplation, anger and worry. Or was that fear?

"Hi," he said simply. "I'm Cyle." He turned to Jenny. "Thanks for bringing her here. You can leave now."

Jenny scoffed. "I'd prefer to stay. Beth has been through a lot today. I think it's better if she has some company."

Cyle's expression hardened. "Leave, please. This is something I have to discuss alone with Beth."

Jenny gave me a worried look. "Are you sure you're going to be okay?"

I looked at the scientist. His brooding demeanour didn't seem threatening. Yes, his arms were still crossed, making it very clear that he didn't want to get too close and personal, but that was fine with me.

"No tests, no probes, no poking?" I asked just to make sure.

Cyle's lips quivered. "None of that. I promise. Just talking."

"Good. I guess that's alright then. Jenny, I'll be fine, but thanks for coming."

She pulled something from her bag and gave it to me. A commstick. "Call me if you need something, no matter what time of day."

Her empathy and care made me all mushy inside. Old Beth may have even got teary. It was nice to know that at least someone on this planet was looking out for me. With Jenny and Ghorr, I had two allies on my side. I was about to find out where on the scale Cyle was located. Friend or enemy.

I was being overly dramatic. Or was I?

Jenny left with a wave. The door closed silently, leaving me alone with the scientist. He still hadn't moved. The longer I looked at him, the more I thought that he seemed uncertain. His gruff posture was just for show.

"Have a seat," he said after a moment's silence. "I'm sorry for having you dragged here like this. We thought you'd been abducted. I've since talked to Ghorr and believe that his intentions were good. Misguided, but not malicious."

"I'm not going back to Obi," I said before he could continue. "If I can't stay with Ghorr, then I'll just wait it out and return to Earth in four weeks."

His eyes widened. "Return to Earth? Is that what you want?"

Was it? I didn't know anymore. Everything was so complicated.

"Maybe," I said honestly. "There's nothing for me back home, but it's starting to look like there's nothing here for me, either."

His arm muscles bulged as he squeezed them tighter around his chest. For a scientist, he was extremely well-built. Not as broad-shouldered as his brother Thorrn, but for human standards, he was still much taller and wider as most guys back on Earth. He would have raised eyebrows if he'd walked through the streets of Glasgow in his green kilt. I realised it matched his emerald eyes. Coincidence or on purpose?

"There is something here for you," he said quietly. "I just don't know how to tell you."

He seemed lost. Tense. As alone as I felt.

I took a deep breath. "Listen. You're a scientist. I'm an engineer. We're both used to thinking rationally. Let's ignore all emotional baggage and simply talk facts. Why did you need me to come here? Did you find out why Obi and I have no chemistry?"

"Chemistry?" he repeated. "What does that have to do with your mating bond?"

"Just a phrase. It means having a connection. Or no connection, in our case."

"Ah. That's easily explained. The two of you aren't mates."

My birthday, Christmas and Hogmanay all happened within a split second. I was free. Obi was officially not my mate. That changed everything. He had no right to even come near me. I'd not have to fight him off any longer.

"But..." Cyle cleared his throat. He'd turned his gaze to the floor, avoiding my eyes. "I found your true mate."

My heart skipped a beat. Another mate. "Is it Ghorr?"

Cyle looked up in shock. "What? No. Not him. Definitely not him. It's not Obi and it's not Ghorr. It's..."

He looked away again. If he hugged himself any tighter, he'd crush his ribcage.

I felt like hugging him. Why did I feel that impulse? I didn't know him. He was a stranger. The only connection I had to him was that he'd matched me with Obi. Well, and he was Jenny's brother-in-law, kind of, but I didn't even know Jenny that well.

I took a step towards him. He didn't look up. His upper hands were under his armpits as if he was trying to prevent himself from touching something. What was going on?

"Who is it?" I asked when he didn't continue.

If men could give birth, this was the expression they'd have.

Cyle licked his lips, cleared his throat, then ran out of things to do to avoid talking. He sighed. "It's me."

7

Cyle

There it was. I'd said the words. Every syllable made my antennae burn even hotter. They were painful now, but I kept myself from touching them. I didn't want to give in to the base instincts our genes predisposed us for. I wasn't an animal. I could resist the urge to run to Beth and take her right here, right now. My cock was aching almost as much as my antennae. It had started as soon as her shuttle had landed outside. The tingles in my mating antennae had announced her presence. There was no doubt any longer. She really was my mate.

And she didn't look happy about it in the slightest.

"Is this some sort of experiment?" she asked incredulously. "Are you testing me? Or are you simply making fun of me?" She turned on her heels and hurried towards the door. "I've had enough."

She was going to leave. My mate was going to leave me.

All restraint forgotten, I leapt up, crossed the room in a flash and stood in front of the door just before Beth reached it. I'd miscalculated my speed somewhat and staggered, reached for the nearest wall, but then Beth was in the way and my hands landed on her chest. Not just anywhere on her chest. On her breasts.

And it felt amazing.

We froze. Her eyes were wide, her lips slightly parted, her nostrils flaring. She didn't move. Didn't step away from my touch. Didn't complain. Didn't do anything. She just looked at me with her beautiful dark eyes and I felt myself drown in her darkness. The emotion hidden within them was too much to bear. I felt things I knew weren't my own. Flashes of images exploded at the back of my mind. Smells. Echoes. Sounds.

I fell into her memories. Some were fragments, others entire scenes playing out before my mind's eye. Many didn't make sense. They were too personal. I lacked the context to understand the significance. But some memories were so clear they felt like my own.

A Peritan male smiling at her, bringing her a bundle of plants that made her happy. The same male, sitting by her side in a simple wooden craft on a lake. I could hear the birds, smell the water. The rational part of my mind wanted to analyse how this was possible, but the images kept coming. Happiness turned into pain and sorrow. I saw how she turned from a carefree young female into someone different, broken inside and hard on the outside. Watching the male die next to her while they were trapped in a crushed metal vehicle made tears spring to my eyes. I felt her pain. I wanted to comfort her, but these were memories, lived already, and there was nothing I could do to ease the depths of her emotions.

I saw her wave goodbye to her planet. Felt her excitement for what lay ahead.

Then the memories turned foggy, dispersed one at a time, until I was back in the present. My antennae no longer burned. My hands were still on her breasts.

How much time had passed?

Her eyes were glassy, as if she was dreaming. Was she seeing my memories? Was the same thing happening to her?

Icy fear gripped me and I finally had the strength to move. I lurched back, as far away from her as possible. Had she seen? Did she know?

She wavered a little before her gaze focused and she was fully present again. She took a step back, clearly driven by the same urge to put some distance between us. Her lips moved, but no sound followed.

I didn't feel ready to speak yet, either. Nobody had mentioned this happening. Not Thorrn, not Eron. None of the other matched males had contacted me to report such an occurrence.

I hadn't been prepared. Now she might know my secret. If she did, she could destroy everything. Not just my work. My life.

I shouldn't have brought her here. I shouldn't have told her. Should have let her leave. Should have...

"Mates," Beth whispered. "We're mates."

It wasn't a question. And why should it be? It was obvious. We'd both felt it. There was no denying it. Beth was my mate, bound to me for the rest of our lives. She was mine.

I should be ecstatic. This was what I'd hoped for. I'd wanted a mate. A female of my own.

One of my antennae itched so much that I found myself scratching it before I even realised. My mind was still a little foggy. I'd not processed all her memories. Too much input with not enough time to analyse, sort, store it.

"Do they hurt?" she asked softly. "I was told that they sometimes do that."

I forced myself to stop scratching and once again wrapped my arms tight around my chest to prevent me from giving in to the urge.

"They itch," I said, my voice not sounding like myself at all. "They no longer hurt."

"I suppose that's good. Well, not good. Better. God, this is awkward." She smiled wryly. "Should we sit down? Ignore the fact that you grabbed my boobs for several minutes?"

I smirked at her choice of words. "Yes. We should. But let's go to the refreshment room. It's more comfortable than this."

I sleepwalked out of the lab, her closely behind me. I could smell her. All my senses were focused on her. And with every step, my cock reminded me just how hard he was. I was grateful that Albyans didn't wear the tight leg garments Peritan males preferred.

The nanomet walls activated as we walked through the dark corridor, displaying gorgeous landscapes from across Albya. Usually, I ignored them, hurrying past with my mind focused on other things, but this time, I tried to look at the walls like it was my first time. As it was for Beth. I couldn't help but admit that Albya was a beautiful planet. Unlike other civilisations, we'd always lived in harmony with nature. Most parts of Albya were still unspoilt. When we were young, Eron, Thorrn and I had explored a lot, travelling to exotic locations. Then the Sleep had happened. Life had never been the same.

That thought reminded me of what was at stake. The Sleep. A cure was more important than my own happiness. Even Beth's happiness. It hurt to even contemplate the only possible solution. But I was a scientist. I thought rationally. I didn't indulge in fairy tales.

By the time we reached the refreshment room, I was back in control. Beth's memories still tingled at the back of my mind, but I had a firm hold on them. I wouldn't be overwhelmed again.

"Is this where you spend time with your colleagues?" Beth asked, looking around the room.

I tried to see it with her eyes. It was bleaker than I'd thought. A food processor was integrated into some cupboards on one side of the room. In the centre were several sofas, most not exactly clean. The wall facing the door showed an image of the ocean, the waves seemingly crashing against the glass.

I dimly remembered that once, there had been a games console in one corner. There'd also been flowers and other decorations.

"I don't come here very often," I admitted. "My assistant brings me food and drinks. I get lost in my work and forget to get my own refreshments. I think others spend their break in here, though."

I didn't even know what a break was. I worked, I slept, I worked, I slept. The trip to Eron's farm had been the first time outside Priomh for what? Two rotations? More?

"I understand that, getting lost in your work," Beth said and sat on one of the sofas.

I'd wished I'd come here earlier to make sure they were clean. Us scientists were all good at keeping our labs tidy - they had to be or our results might be spoilt - but not everything else.

She took a deep breath. "Let's talk about the elephant in the room. What just happened? Did you see my memories? Because I saw yours."

My stomach clenched and bile rose in my throat. I didn't want to have this conversation. My body and mind ached for her, but this was all sorts of wrong.

"Did you see?" I burst out. "Do you know?"

She frowned at me. "You need to be more specific. I saw a lot of things. And you still haven't answered my questions."

Of course. She wouldn't know the significance of what she'd witnessed. She didn't have the cultural knowledge Albyans had. I wasn't even sure how much the Peritan females had been taught about the Sleep.

Maybe I shouldn't push any further. Even if she'd seen, she wasn't aware that it was a secret. But what if she talked about it with other people? Told them my secret? No. I had to tell her. She had to know.

"Maybe you should sit down," she said. "You look like you're about to keel over."

She was right. I didn't feel good at all.

I dropped onto the sofa furthest away from Beth. Too close and I might lose control. I had to think. Stay focused. Ignore her scent that was getting stronger, driving me crazy.

"Do you want a glass of water? Not that I have any idea how to get you one." She laughed. "I thought living on the Starlight would have prepared me for your alien technology, but it turns out it didn't. It's all so different."

I pointed at the food processor. "This is for larger meals. The programming will be similar to what you're used to from the Starlight. For drinks and snacks, use the walls. Ah. No. You can't. They're not attuned to you. But if they were, you could use the nanomet walls."

This wasn't what we should be talking about. My antennae were starting to ache again, reminding me that my mate was ever so close. Not that I needed the reminder. My cock was still hard, still pushing against my kilt, especially now that I was seated. Could balls explode? From the way they felt, it seemed likely.

Beth was looking at me in silence. How much had those beautiful dark eyes seen? How far had she strayed into my soul?

I pulled out my commstick and activated the secrecy function. A light pressure against my eardrums signalled that the room was now completely soundproof. Nobody would be able to listen in.

"What did you do?" Beth asked, rubbing her ears. One of them was badly scarred.

"I made sure that this conversation will stay between us. There's something important I need to tell you. It will also help explain why I can't be your mate."

Her shock hurt more than any weapon ever could. She staggered to her feet, betrayal reflecting across her face.

"You don't want to be with me?" she whispered.

What the sgid was I doing? I was hurting her. She'd been through a lot. She'd lost her first mate. She'd barely survived herself. She'd been wrongly matched to a male. When she'd sought help from another, I'd sent the enforcers, traumatising her yet again. And now I was rejecting her.

I was a monster. I didn't deserve to be with her.

"Why?" she asked quietly. Her emotions no longer showed. She was putting up her walls. Shutting me out before she'd even let me in. I didn't want her to lock herself away. I'd seen her memories, felt her pain. This was wrong.

"I made a vow," I said quickly. "I promised that I wouldn't take a mate until I found a cure for the Sleep. I can't get distracted from my work. I have to find a way for our females to wake up."

She stared at me for a long time.

"Why you?" she asked finally. "Why do you put the sole responsibility for finding a cure on your shoulders? You aren't the only scientist on Albya. You deserve to have a life, just like everyone else."

Suddenly, her eyes widened. "I saw. In your memories. Is that why?"

I nodded. "My father caused the Sleep. It's my duty as his son to cure it."

8

Beth

I no longer knew what to think or feel. I wanted to hug Cyle. Slap him. Run away before he could hurt my brittle heart.

His memories had been night and day. The first ones had been full of happiness and excitement. I'd seen him as a young boy, then as a teenager. He'd had a happy childhood. He'd wanted for nothing. Already, his thinking had been analytical, but his behaviour had been less controlled. He'd had the courage to take risks, even if that meant having to fess up to his mistakes.

But then, the Sleep. It crept into his memories like a dark fog, pushing away all joy. I watched as he shook his prone mother, begging for her to wake up. I saw how his father was no longer at home, spending all day and night in his lab, searching for a cure. Just like his son now.

And then, the scene that still made me tremble. Cyle's father, his face streaked with tears, breaking down into a sobbing mess. Telling his son how he was the cause of the Sleep. How he'd tried to increase fertility rates and had instead created the biggest catastrophe ever to befall Albya. After his confession, Cyle's father slowly walked away. Moments later, an explosion. Fire everywhere. Smoke. Cyle running into the lab, trying to get to his parents, but it was too late.

They both perished in the same instant. His father in the explosion of his making, his mother because they were mates and linked. Just like all sleeping females, she died when her mate did. Cyle's father had committed murder and suicide in the same moment.

The scenes after were even more heart-breaking. Cyle became reclusive, weighed down by the secret. He never told his brother Thorrn about it. He let him believe that the fire at the lab had been an accident. But I could feel how hard it was on him to lie. Cyle was all about the infallibility of data. His research was flawless, but his mind was dark with shame.

When the memories had scrolled along in my mind, I'd wanted to hug him tight, tell him that none of it had been his fault. He wasn't his father. He'd had no part in it. On the contrary, he was sacrificing every living moment to make up for his father's mistakes. No one, no matter how young or old, should have to do that.

But I'd not been able to move. I'd been trapped in the stream of memories, forcing me to watch. Cyle became older. He rarely left the lab. He was obsessed.

The gloom only started lifting when he found Earth. Peritus, as he called it. His trip to our planet was the first ray of happiness he'd experienced in at least a decade. I'd thought I'd walked in darkness for a long time. It was nothing compared to Cyle.

And now, here we were. I'd seen flashes of his life. I knew him even though he hadn't told me any of it himself. And I was convinced that he'd seen my memories. He'd not admitted to it yet. But I could see it in his eyes. He knew me. Maybe better than anyone else ever had. Depending on what he'd seen, he might know things I never told a soul. Not even my husband. It made me feel guilty. If I hadn't told the man I'd hoped to spend my life with, then a stranger shouldn't know, either. Not even if he was my mate.

I realised I was still standing. How long since I'd got up, intending to rush from the room?

I no longer knew what to do. I sat down again with a sigh.

"Would you like a drink?" Cyle asked cautiously.

"If you're talking about something stronger than tea or water, yes. I could do with a drink."

He got a tiny bottle from a cupboard, only enough to fill two shot glasses. The liquid was a murky grey, not exactly appetising. When he handed me a glass, I gave it a sniff. Aniseed. Maybe. An alien version of it, anyway.

"Slàinte Mhath," Cyle said and downed his glass in one go.

Foregoing all caution, I did the same. The alcohol burned my throat, but then a soothing warmth spread through my stomach, making up for it. I coughed, then held out my glass.

"More?"

Cyle shook his head. "Not yet. I don't know what effect it'll have on you. It's strong and Peritans are fragile."

I didn't like being called fragile. I'd been broken, then put together again, but the seams that had mended the shards had made me stronger.

I kept my glass in the air, waiting for him to refill it.

Cyle sighed. "Are you sure?"

When I nodded, he rummaged in the cupboard again and produced another bottle. This one was a little bigger than the first.

"This is Thorrn's favourite," he said when he poured me the drink. "Let's see if you like it."

The liquid was golden, like whisky, but it smelled floral. This time, I took a smaller sip first. I was starting to feel the effect of the alcohol already. He'd been right. It was strong.

"It's pretty good," I said and took another sip. "But I preferred the first."

Cyle's lips turned into the smallest smile. "That was my favourite. But I've run out. I haven't drunk any for... a long time. It addles the mind. I can't afford distractions."

"Today, you can. I think we both deserve it after what's happened."

He nodded. "I suppose you're right. It's not like you find your mate every day."

The word made a shiver run down my back, ending in my lady parts. Mate. How did those four simple letters turn me on?

Cyle had said he didn't want me. He'd made a vow. If I was a decent human being, I'd leave him to it. Leave while I still could. Give him the life of research and service he wanted.

But meeting Obi had shown me how much I craved a partner. A *mate*. The absence of feelings between us had been so painful that it had left no doubt about the hole within me, a hole that yearned to be filled. Cyle was the answer. I'd met him half an hour ago and yet I craved him like nothing else.

He emptied his glass in one go and filled it right away. I gulped down my own golden flower brandy - or whatever it was - and held out my glass again. When he leant down to fill it, I got a whiff of his musky scent. Male. Very male.

And so very familiar. I was starting to feel warm all over and it had nothing to do with the alcohol. My body was aching for him. I wanted Cyle.

He'd only touched me once so far. By accident, his hands on my boobs. It wasn't how I'd wanted our first touch to go. I wanted him to caress my skin, cover me in kisses, before revealing whatever he was hiding under his kilt and claiming me.

The Albyans on the Starlight had made a big secret of their downstairs anatomy. No sex ed classes for us. And no peek allowed. His was the first Albyan cock I'd see. And I would see it. He was my mate. He was mine.

I carelessly put my glass on the sofa and got up, surprising him. I wrapped my arms around him, revelling in his warmth. Hard planes of muscle stiffened beneath my touch. I should have stepped back, should have apologised, but the woozy warmth in my mind made me continue. I pressed my face against his chest, breathing in his scent. I couldn't put my finger on what he smelled off. Something earthy, slightly peppery. It was the most delicious scent in the universe.

Finally, he moved. His hands - well, two of them - came to rest on my head. I was wearing my usual headwrap, although it had come slightly loose at some point during the night. It wouldn't take much for it to fall off, exposing my burnt scalp, my hideous scars.

I wanted him to ask to remove his hands from my head, but then his lower set of arms wrapped around my waist and I was pushed against him. He held me so tight it was hard to breathe. As if he was scared to let me go. In return, I clung to him, tightening my own grip. It felt *right*. Everything about him was familiar. His scent, his touch, even his heartbeat.

His erection pressed against me, but in this moment, sex wasn't what I needed. I wanted more of him. I wanted him to give himself to me. Open up. Let me in. Bind himself to me so that I could be sure that he'd never leave me. Never push me away like he'd threatened.

"Don't," I whispered.

"Don't what?" His voice was husky.

"Don't let go."

His hands moved from my head down to my cheeks and he pushed me back ever so slightly so that I could look up at him. His emerald eyes were blazing with emotion.

"Never."

He sealed the words with a kiss. His lips were on mine before I saw him move. I closed my eyes and returned the kiss, opening my lips to him. He no longer held back.

No more doubts.

No more restraint.

Reality could go fuck itself.

I kissed him as if my life depended on it. Our tongues met, danced, while our breaths went as one. His hands roamed across my back, one slipping beneath my shirt. Thank god I'd changed from a dress into a shirt and skirt. Feeling his hands on my naked skin was everything. And he was still kissing me like there was no tomorrow.

For a moment, life was as it was supposed to be. The stars had aligned themselves and shone upon us. For a small moment.

Until a tear dropped onto my cheek and I realised it had been too good to be true.

9

Cyle

It was the stuff of dreams. Beth was a miracle. Holding her in my arms, kissing her, was more than I could have asked for.

Her slender body fit mine perfectly. We were made for each other. Mates.

But the longer we kissed, the faster my conscience returned. It had been dimmed by the uisge beatha and Beth's touch, but now it was back, screaming at me to stop.

I'd made a vow. I couldn't have Beth. Not yet.

The thought of not having her by my side broke my heart. My eyes stung at the same time as my antennae started burning with fury. A single tear escaped, falling onto Beth's cheek.

She stilled. Our lips were still fused together, but she'd stopped moving, even stopped breathing.

How such a miniscule group of hydrogen and oxygen molecules could destroy everything.

The tear was the signal to stop. This had gone far enough.

"You said forever," Beth whispered. "And now you're already changing your mind?"

I groaned. I wanted her so much it hurt. But I had to stay in control.

"I meant it," I said, my voice hoarse and dry. "But not yet. Not now. I have to find the cure. Then I can be the mate you deserve."

She moved backwards, but I didn't let go of her. I couldn't.

"And how long will that be? Months? Years? Will we both die before you even find a cure? This doesn't make sense, Cyle, and you know it."

She'd said my name. For the first time. I liked how it sounded in her Peritan accent. A little harsher, but I could listen to her saying my name all day long. And all night.

Not helping. I wanted to push her away and at the same time keep her pressed against me. Now I knew why Thorrn kept carrying his mate around. It was hard not to touch her.

"I can't." I had to force the words out. "If I give in, if I claim you, I won't be able to focus. You'll be all that's on my mind. I want to give you all my attention. I want to spend every click with you. But I have to think of more than just my needs. Our species is dying and I can't rest until I find the cure." I sighed deeply. "Until now, I've never considered giving up my mission. Know that you make me want to throw it all away. You're so close to breaking my conviction."

Her eyes shone with tears. "I can't go. I won't leave you. I only just found you."

There was no way around it. I'd have to break the delicate thread spun between us.

"You don't know me," I said and finally let go of her. I stepped back fast as if touching her would burn me. "This is an illusion, nothing more. We're more than our genes. We can control this temptation."

"We," she scoffed, her smile fading. "You mean *you*. I have no desire to resist. When I met Obi, I felt nothing for him, but I saw all the other women react to their matches. Their bodies leant towards each other without them even realising. And now that's exactly how it is with you. I won't give this up. I won't."

"You have to," I said as gently as I could. "I can't give you what you need."

She looked close to punching me. It would be in her right. I deserved it.

Every single male in Albya would be grateful to get a mate. Me? I refused the match. I was an absolute idiot. When my brother found out, he'd have a few choice words to say. And Jenny, his mate...I was scared of her fury. She was a bundle of feminine energy ready to strike whoever went against her and the other Peritan females. She wouldn't understand. Neither would Thorrn. They didn't know what our father had done. They didn't feel the guilt I'd been carrying around ever since I discovered the truth.

My father had been selfish. When he'd burned the lab, himself in it, he'd destroyed all his research. Any data that could have helped me find a cure was gone. I still didn't understand why he'd done it. End his life, yes. I got it. He'd sentenced our species to extinction. But why destroy the lab? He could have found other ways to kill himself. And he must have known that my mother would die the instant he did. In all the years since that horrible moment, I'd still not found an answer. He'd loved her. I'd expected him to fight for her, not give up on both of them.

"I give you a month," Beth suddenly said, ripping me from my thoughts. "One month to find a cure. After that, I'm organising the handfasting ceremony and you're mine."

"One month?" I echoed. "That's not enough. It could take years. The data is promising, there might be a cure hidden within you Peritans, but I need more time."

"One month. Twenty-seven Albyan days. Or wait, I'll be generous. You get an Earth month. Thirty days. And I'm not saying you have to stop your research after. Not at all. But I won't wait longer than that to officially become your mate."

The burning heat in my antennae lessened to a warm tingle. They approved. Was I really going to let these two tiny appendages dictate my life?

I looked down at Beth and decided that yes, I would. Her deal gave me a goal, an ultimatum. A month was different now than it had been a rotation ago. Back then, we'd not discovered Peritus. We didn't know that there were compatible females across the stars. Now, everything was different.

Maybe I could do this.

Beth was encouragement enough.

"One month," I agreed. "And we will meet once a day for lunch."

A smile spread across her face. "Will there be kissing?"

"Are you trying to kill me, lass?"

The smile turned into a wicked grin. "It's you who's making me wait. The least you could do is sweeten the deal."

And I did. I pushed away all doubts and worries and kissed her like she deserved it.

The next morning, Beth appeared at the lab with ten females in tow. Even June had arrived with Eron by her side.

"They're all eager to help," she explained. "Prod us as much as you like."

"But no probing like in the films," one female with bright blue hair warned. "Or my mate will kill you."

"He's an enforcer," one of the others whispered. "He probably really would."

I stared at the gaggle of females. I wasn't ready to examine them all. I needed help. I reached for my commstick, but Vhom was already hurrying down the corridor.

"What's going on?" he asked breathlessly.

"Call in everyone. Hag, Kloyd, Beerd, every sgidding scientist we've ever had. I don't care what other plans they have. We need everyone here."

Vhom nodded. He didn't know about the one-month ultimatum yet. Beth and I had only separated a few hours ago, her taking a shuttle to her hotel, me sleeping on my bed in the lab. I was bone-wearily tired, but seeing them all volunteering to be studied renewed my energy.

"What about Jafar?" Vhom asked warily.

I growled. Jafar was trouble. I'd called him a friend until he'd betrayed us on the way back to Albya. Jenny had been hurt and both Thorrn and I had been busy keeping her alive. Jafar had used the opportunity to tell his relative on the Council of Elders about her, potentially condemning her to be used as a science experiment. Luckily, we'd managed to negotiate and Jenny was now a voluntary test subject under my own supervision. She'd never come to harm. But Jafar hadn't cared about that. He'd been so desperate to get his own mate that he'd been willing to sacrifice Jenny.

If only he wasn't such a brilliant scientist.

"Call him in," I huffed. "But keep an eye on him."

"I won't leave his side," Vhom promised.

"Good. I'll make a plan of who does what. Let's turn this into a challenge. We're going to find a cure for the Sleep within the next month."

Vhom gasped. "A month?"

"Let's make it thirty days," I said, giving Beth a wink.

She beamed. My cock stirred when I remembered our parting kiss last night. Well, technically this morning. I couldn't wait for lunchtime. But first, I had ten other females to deal with.

"Follow me," I told them and led them into the heart of the lab building, my steps lively with hope.

Beth

It was fascinating to see Cyle in action. I stayed by his side and watched as he organised teams, assigned students to help out experienced scientists, handed out tasks.

Jenny reassured everyone that the tests were non-invasive and painless, except for when they took blood samples. I knew some people didn't like hospitals, but for me, the hospital had been a place I'd felt safe. After the accident, everything had been chaos. When I woke from my coma, the doctors and nurses treated me like someone they'd known for weeks – which they had, in a way. I used the time there to grieve and recover. The difficult part was stepping back into the real world and dealing with all the official crap my husband's death and my long absence from work had caused.

No, hospitals weren't the problem. Everything else was.

"I really don't like needles," Kate complained.

I was about to persuade her that needles were small hollow rods that meant no harm, but Jenny was faster, taking her aside.

Eventually, every woman was in a separate room with at least one scientist assigned to her. I didn't understand most of what Cyle told them to do, but I trusted him to know what he was doing. He was Albya's First Scientist, after all. Everyone treated him with respect, almost deference, making me realise just how important he really was.

He took his assistant Vhom and me to his own lab, the same room I'd first met him last night. My lips tingled at the memory of our first kiss. For a moment, I felt his hands on my breasts again. I squeezed my thighs together, fighting my arousal. I really hoped he would find the cure before I went crazy with need.

"There's something I wanted to discuss," Vhom said as soon as the door closed behind us, turning foggy to give us privacy. "But I got a little distracted by all the females."

Cyle chuckled and shot me a look. "They have that effect."

Vhom was a young male, one of the youngest I'd seen so far. There were no children on Albya since no female had been able to give birth since the start of the Sleep. He had to be very good at his job to be Cyle's assistant at such a young age. I supposed the Sleep hadn't just robbed Albyan females of their waking lives, but also every child of their childhood. Girls would fall asleep as soon as they reached adulthood, while boys grew up without their mothers.

"I found something yesterday, but I wanted to verify it before I told you," Vhom began. "I checked on our control group and noticed a change in their brain wave patterns. All twenty of them have altered patterns."

I watched in fascination as a myriad of emotions raced across Cyle's face.

"Altered how?" he asked after a long pause.

Vhom went to a circular table in the centre of the room and pressed his hand against it. A holographic sphere appeared above it. I had no idea what he was doing, but Cyle seemed to understand the data he was showing us.

"Throw it on the big screen," he commanded.

Graphs, diagrams, numbers and unfamiliar symbols appeared on the wall to my right. The entire wall had turned into a screen. I loved this alien tech.

Cyle crossed his arms as he studied the data while Vhom stood close behind him, waiting patiently.

"What are we seeing?" I whispered to him.

"Until recently, the brain waves of the females in our control group matched those of someone in a deep coma. Enough activity to tell us that they're still alive and not brain dead, but not enough for us to know if they're aware. And now-"

"They're dreaming," Cyle interrupted. "Our females are dreaming." He ran a hand through his hair before clamping his fingers around one antenna. "This changes everything. Vhom, did you check with any of our partner institutes? Did any of them see the same transformation?"

"No, they didn't. Which makes me think that something here is influencing our female patients."

Cyle nodded. "Jenny has been here regularly. The samples we've taken from her are stored in the room next to where we care for the females." He turned to me. "Beth, come with me."

He hurried out of the lab and I had to run to keep up with him. His elation was infectious. Not just because waking the Albyan females meant Cyle would become my mate.

The twenty women each lay in a glass pod, their expressions serene, their bodies hidden under soft white blankets. They reminded me of the Sleeping Beauty fairy tale. Sleeping yet unable to be woken until the moment was right.

The room was bright and welcoming, not at all like what I'd imagined. Pictures hung on the walls and large plant pots stood in the corners, adding to the homely atmosphere.

Above each pod, a holographic display showed the woman's vitals. Cyle rushed to the closest one and ran his hands through the data, increasing it in size.

"Impossible," he muttered. "How is this happening?"

He went to another pod, and another, his expression turning more intrigued with every one he passed.

"Beth, come closer. Put your hands on the pod."

I did as he asked. To my surprise, the glass was warm and felt a little soft, like thick gelatine. Not glass after all.

Even I recognised the spike in the otherwise rhythmic lines on the display. I was having an effect on the woman. My mere presence changed her brain waves.

"Impossible," Cyle repeated. "How is this happening? The females are hermetically separated from the environment. That rules out any pheromones or other particles you might emit. How do they know you're here? How can you change their brain waves?"

I had no answers for him.

Cyle pulled out his commstick and pressed some buttons. "Thorrn. Take Jenny and go to the closest

Sleep facility. Have them monitor the females' brain data and send it to me. Quickly."

He ended the call before his brother even had a chance to respond.

Cyle put his hands on mine. Another spike appeared on the monitor, even larger.

"How?" he whispered. "What am I missing?"

I smiled at him. "I'm starting to think you won't need an entire month."

I spent most of the next three days with the sleeping women. My presence stimulated them in ways the scientists didn't understand. I talked to the females, telling them random things about my life on Earth. When I ran out of things to say, I resorted to reciting poems and fairy tales. I sent a mental thank you note to my English literature teacher who'd punished any infraction by making the entire class learn a new poem by heart. I knew dozens and dozens of poems, everything from sonnets to limericks to epics. I even managed to recite some of the Canterbury tales, but when my memory failed, I improvised and simply made up the rest of the story.

When I needed to eat or sleep, one of the other human women took over. They were all just as excited as me.

Cyle had sent some of them to other labs and care facilities. The results were always the same. We had an immediate effect on the sleeping Albyans. The problem was, none of the scientists understood why.

Cyle's enthusiasm turned into frustration, then exhaustion. He met me for lunch as promised, but he was distracted and barely focused on our conversation.

"Oi," I snapped when he didn't answer the question I'd asked a minute ago. "Stop brooding. You need a break. When did you last sleep?"

He evaded my gaze, which told me everything I needed to know.

"You can't solve this if you're exhausted. I promise you the women won't wake up while you get a few hours of sleep. And if they do, I'll wake you."

Cyle shook his head. "I can't. I tried to sleep, but I just can't. I need to work. They depend on me."

Such a ridiculous man. I checked he'd emptied his plate – I was convinced that lunch with me was the only regular meal he was getting – and got up, dragging him from the refreshment room. He let himself be led without protest, yet another sign of how tired he was.

We stopped in front of his bed. Just like my bed at the hotel, it was a lot bigger than what you'd find on Earth, accommodating Albyans' larger bodies.

"Lie down," I commanded.

"Now?"

"Now. You need to sleep."

He crossed all four of his arms. "This is ridiculous. I have too much to do."

It was time to resort to more drastic measures. I pushed him back as hard as I could. He didn't move an inch. Bloody hell. I'd underestimated his strength.

His lips quivered into a smirk. "You're being violent."

"Just doing what's necessary. Will you lie down on your own volition, or do I need to get your brother? I'm sure he'd love to force you. I'm told he's a lot stronger than you."

Cyle glared at me. "Do. Not. Involve. My. Brother."

"Then don't be a baby and lie down. You know what? I'm going to do the same. That way, I know that you're not secretly getting up as soon as I leave the room."

"You're getting into bed with me?" His anger changed into something else. The same need I felt mirrored across his face. It made me all gooey inside.

"Yes. And if you don't lie down right away, I'm going to take my clothes off."

"I'm not sure if that's a threat or a promise." His voice turned into dark chocolate. I could listen to him forever. That was the kind of voice that could make me do anything he wanted.

"It's you who's stopping us from taking the next step." I made sure the door had turned opaque before lifting the hem of my shirt ever so slightly. My belly was one of the few places on my body that wasn't heavily scarred. But even if it had been, I felt no shame when in Cyle's presence. It had taken me months to walk around in public with my scars on full display. I'd taken a course in how best to cover them with makeup, but that had never worked out as it should.

With Cyle, it was different. I suddenly felt like I had before the accident. Confident in my own skin. I could imagine stripping in front of him, showing him my flawed body.

I was so very tempted. His hungry expression told me I wasn't the only one thinking along those lines. He looked at me with a predatory glance that seemed to undress me even with my clothes still on.

I put a hand on his chest. "Do you want it?"

Cyle cupped my cheeks with two hands while his other two rested on my hips. He held me in place for a while, simply staring down at me with hunger. Then he took a deep breath and stepped back, crossing his arms in front of his chest again.

"I can't. But I agree to sleep with you." He almost choked. "Not with you. Not in that way. Sleep in the same bed. If you want. But you don't have to."

And here he was again, my babbling scientist. The switch had been surprisingly fast. If he found his cure, would his melty chocolate voice stay for good?

He finally lay on the bed, his back against the wall to make space for me. I decided to keep on my clothes. This time.

As much as I wanted to look at him, I decided he needed his sleep without any distractions. I turned my back to him, facing the room. A cool draught hit my arms and goosebumps broke out across my skin.

Without warning, Cyle wrapped his arms around me and pulled me against him.

"Just so you don't get cold," he muttered gruffly.

Sure. If he said so.

His skin was warm and I soaked in his heat. I closed my eyes, listening to his even breaths as they became slower.

It was our first time in bed together, but not exactly how I'd planned it.

Next time, I told myself.

Once he'd found a cure, we'd spend at least a week in bed. Without clothes.

11

Cyle

Time passed quickly. Way too quickly. At the halfway point of Beth's deadline, I still didn't know how exactly her presence affected the Albyan females.

Beth forced me to sleep every day. Or night. The days blurred into each other. There were no windows in the belly of the lab building to show what time it was outside. I worked until I got too tired or until Beth came to bring me to bed.

It was strangely endearing. I found myself faking a yawn to get her to pull me towards my office. Her body fit against mine perfectly. She called it spooning and kept insisting that it would feel even better if we were to take off our clothes. I had no doubts about that.

My cock was permanently erect. The petals vibrated incessantly and I wasn't sure if this would have long term effects on my dick's health. Beth didn't know about that problem, of course. She'd teasingly asked me what I was hiding under my kilt and I'd given her a similarly mischievous response. I'd once caught her chatting with some of the other Peritan females, one of which was drawing a shaky depiction of an Albyan cock on her commstick. It made sense that the females were comparing notes – they were in a completely new, alien environment after all – but I hoped Beth wouldn't end up with preconceptions.

Albyan under-the-kilt anatomy differed slightly. We had different numbers of petals and our stalks' shape varied from clan to clan. I had five petals, one more than Thorrn, which had driven him crazy in our youth. He'd been the brawnier one of the two of us and he'd assumed that would mean his cock would be bigger, too. I grinned to myself. It still was a sore point for him.

"Cyle!"

Vhom came running into my office, almost crashing into the holobase in the centre of the room.

"She's waking up!"

I blinked at him. It took me a moment to process his words. "Who?"

"My mother! Come quickly!"

He was gone before I could even get up from my chair. I ran a hand through my tousled hair. When had I last taken a shower? Not that it mattered.

A female waking up. It couldn't be.

I raced through the building. Beth waited by the door to the control group's room, bouncing with excitement.

"I was just about to get you," she said cheerily. "Vhom's mother muttered something. We think she's close to waking up."

Two Peritan females stood next to the pod in question. Vhom had opened the lid, holding his mother's hand. Usually, I would have chastised him, but in this moment, the chance of having her be cured of the Sleep was more important than the small risk of exposing her to germs.

"Report," I commanded.

Kloyd, an elderly scientist who would have retired by now if not for the Sleep, handed me his commstick. "Take a look yourself."

I scrolled through the data. I felt my eyes widening with every new bit of information I processed. The female's brain waves had altered to the point of now resembling normal sleep. Not just that. *Light* sleep that someone could easily be woken from. Technically, the sound of all of us stomping around her should have woken her by now.

"She squeezed my hand!" Vhom shouted before lowering his voice. "And look. Her lips are moving."

I hurried closer to the pod. He was right. Her lips quivered as if she was trying to speak. I pulled up one of her eyelids. Reactive to light. That was a good sign.

"If you can hear us, squeeze your son's hand."

I could have sworn her lips formed the word 'son'.

"She did it," Vhom cheered. "She's weak, but she definitely squeezed."

I'd waited for this moment ever since I'd started my work at this institute, from a lab assistant all the way up to becoming First Scientist of Albya. But now that it was happening, the end of the Sleep, I didn't know what to do. There had been plans, once, when we still had hope that the Sleep was just a temporary illness that would pass quickly. Months had turned to years and those plans had started gathering dust.

I should probably inform the Council of Elders.

Beth stabbed her finger into my side, getting my attention. "Hey, over here. This woman looks like she's waking up, too."

The screen above the female's pod identified her as Lydda of Clan MacCrach. I pressed my hand onto the pod, letting it read my palm print. It opened with a hiss, revealing the prone body of Lydda. Her red hair pooled around her head like the evening sun. She was past her prime, but the fact that she was still alive meant she had a mate waiting for her. We'd have to notify him as soon as we knew more.

Lydda's fingers twitched. In a fit of inspiration, I told Beth to take her hand.

As soon as Beth touched Lydda, the female's eyes fluttered open. I couldn't believe what I was seeing. Was I still in bed, dreaming?

I hastily checked all of her vitals. They were completely different from what they'd been only yesterday. She really was waking up.

But would she stay awake?

That question made me shiver. I didn't even want to consider that option. Maybe we shouldn't tell anyone yet. Raising hopes only to shatter them again wasn't fair for the relatives.

"Can you hear me?" I asked Lydda.

She looked at me with glassy eyes, then moved her head ever so slightly. A nod.

I wanted to scream with joy. Instead, I leant down and hugged Beth to my chest. She squealed in surprise, then laughed and let me cuddle her.

"First Scientist, over here." Kloyd's amused voice cut through my happiness, reminding me of my role. I had to get a grip on my emotions.

"They're all waking," Kloyd reported, pointing at the other pods. "We need more people. Healers to make sure the females are healthy. Mind healers to assess their psychological state. And-"

"I know," I interrupted. "I'll put you in charge of communicating with the necessary agencies. Don't call their families yet. We want to be sure the females are going to stay awake before we raise their hopes. Maybe inform the institutes that have been visited by Peritans. Their females might be waking up, too."

I turned to Beth. "Call the other Peritans, please. It might make the process faster if they're all here. Jenny will want to know, too."

My commstick vibrated. Eron. I was about to reject the call when a message popped up above his face.

My sister is waking.

I took his call immediately.

"She's waking up!" Eron shouted without greeting. "I just arrived at the facility and she's got her eyes open. She can't speak yet, but she's trying."

"We see the same thing with the females in our care." I noticed I was smiling. Not just smiling. Grinning widely. "Can you find out if it's the same for the other females at your sister's facility? They weren't visited by your mate, so it'll be interesting to see if there's a change in their condition."

Eron grumbled something about not wanting to leave his sister's side, but then agreed. "I'll call you as soon as I know more."

Someone coughed. A female. I disregarded the sound as coming from one of the Peritans until my instincts made me turn around. One of the Albyan females was trying to sit up within her closed pod.

Things descended into chaos. The room was too small for all the healers, scientists, assistants and Peritan females, so we wheeled half of the pods into the neighbouring lab.

The next few hours passed in a blur. I hurried from female to female, Beth always by my side. I wasn't sure I could have done it without her. I was used to sitting in my lab, not interacting with dozens if not hundreds of people. They all looked at me for answers. And I had none.

Two males turned up, having felt their mate bond react. Their antennae had turned bright red, a clear indication that something was going on. Their hopeful, desperate expressions at the sight of their waking females made me feel guilty.

They'd been deprived of their females' company for a generation. Yet here I was, rejecting my own mate because of misguided rules I'd set for myself. I was a sgidding idiot.

When I caught Beth leaning against a wall, her eyelids drooping, I scooped her into my arms and carried her to my lab. I sighed in relief when the door closed behind us. Silence.

"You can let me down now," Beth laughed. "As much as I like being hugged by you, getting carried around the building goes a little far. I have a reputation to protect."

"A reputation?"

"You've not noticed?" She chuckled. "I should have known. You're a brilliant man but you're not very good at reading people, are you. They all revere you for discovering us humans as compatible mates. Somehow, that is rubbing off on how they see me. They treat me with way more respect than the other women. Don't get me wrong, everyone's very polite to all of us, but the others have commented on how I get a different treatment."

"I had no idea," I admitted.

"I know. It's what makes you so adorable." She wriggled in my arms. "Now let me down. I need something to eat."

I only increased my hold on her. "Let me do my duties as your mate and provide you with sustenance."

I ignored her squealing and wiggling while I had the food processor make her a Peritan-style meal. Jenny had programmed several dishes into the database, but since I didn't know what they were, I simply picked the first one on the list.

"Are you going to put me down so I can eat?" Beth demanded when the food processor spat out a bowl of something that looked like pale worms drenched in blood.

"No. I'm going to feed you."

"I'm not a baby," the protested, renewing her struggles.

"No, you're not. You're my mate. I have ignored my duties as your male for too long. I will make up for it, starting with feeding you like Ka'pa fed Ma'pa."

"I didn't think you were religious."

I wasn't surprised she knew the Albyan origin myth. They must have taught her on the Starlight.

"I am not. But it gives me a good excuse to do this."

I gathered some of the worms on a spork and held it to her plump lips. She locked eyes with me, glaring at me for just long enough to convey her message, then she grinned and opened her mouth.

It turned out eating these Peritan worms required a great deal of slurping. Red blood-sauce soon covered her cheeks and my chest.

She never took her eyes off me. With every sporkful of food she took from me, my cock grew harder. It was such a primal action that stirred something deep within me. I was taking care of my female. Feeding her. Protecting her. Something I should have done from the start.

So much had gone wrong between us. It was time to make up for all my mistakes and mend our mate bond.

12

Beth

I expected Cyle to return to work as soon as my bowl was empty, so I ate as slowly as I could. Considering the chaos outside the room, it was selfish, but I couldn't help it. I was craving his presence, couldn't get enough of it.

I had no idea how or why he'd made me spaghetti Bolognese, but it was strangely soothing to eat some familiar food.

He held me tightly as if he was afraid I'd disappear. After two weeks of being pushed away every time I tried to get close, this was an unexpected turn of events. Now that I was sitting on his lap, I knew how hard he was under his kilt. In any other situation, I would have taken advantage of this position, but I was all too aware of how many people were relying on Cyle today. This was a short moment of quiet before we had to go back into the pandemonium caused by the waking of the Albyan women.

"You need to eat something, too," I told Cyle after swallowing the final sporkful of spaghetti. "You're the most important person in the building. Probably on the planet, at this very moment. We can't have you faint from hunger."

"I have a very different hunger I'd like to sate," he whispered huskily. "But I've been thinking."

"Of course you have. Does your brain ever stop?"

"No. Does yours?"

He didn't wait for an answer.

"We have enough scientists and healers looking after the females just now. What we need are answers. Will they stay awake? What changed? How can we replicate this for all Albyans without you and the other Peritans having to visit every single facility? Is this something we can turn into a drug to be administered? Will the females fall asleep again once they're no longer in contact with Peritans? Will-"

I put a finger on his lips to silence him. "I get it. Lots of questions. Not enough answers. If I was to look at this from an engineering point of view, I'd inspect the smallest parts, then work my way up. Sometimes, a single brick can be the issue of a house's collapse. Not that I build houses, but you get the idea."

"The smallest parts," he repeated slowly. "You're right. I will get cellular samples from the woken females and compare them to samples we took before Jenny's arrival. Even though I'd much rather stay like this, you in my lap, your lips so close I could kiss them if only I bent down."

"There is an ancient Earth tradition. A kiss for good luck. Maybe if you kiss me, you'll find all the answers."

He smirked. "This tradition seems very convenient. I'd hate to deprive you of your Peritan rituals."

The moment his lips touched mine, heat erupted all over my body. My nipples grew hard and a deep throbbing started between my thighs. The effect he was having on me with a simple kiss was ridiculous. His tongue swiped against mine, bringing with it his signature taste. I moaned before I could hold back.

Cyle froze. "Did I hurt you?" he asked, pulling away.

"On the contrary."

"That sound you made..."

"A good sound."

"Oh." He ran a finger along my bottom lip. "Should I try to make you create that sound again?"

Always the scientist.

"Yes. I challenge you."

He gave me a wicked smile. "Challenge accepted."

He kissed me again and this time, he slipped a hand under my shirt. His palm was soft against my skin as he drew slow circles around my lower back. He may as well have touched my pussy. I was putty beneath his touch. Another moan broke from my throat.

All too quickly, he stopped the kiss. Breathless and flushed, I looked up at him. I knew this wasn't the time, but I wished it was. I wanted him so much. Needed him. Craved him with every cell in my body. Maybe he should research that. How it was possible for me to crave him this much.

"I need to work," he whispered with a sigh. "But you should stay here. Take a break. Peritan bodies are-"

"Fragile," I completed the sentence for him. "You keep saying that. Yet we're the ones who're somehow healing your women. Maybe not as fragile as you all thought."

"Fragile. Broken. Incomplete."

He was no longer looking at me. His gaze had turned inwards and I knew he was thinking hard.

I climbed off his lap and left him to his science. I didn't think he even noticed when I slipped out of the room. His nerdiness was adorable.

I found Jenny with the first Albyan woman who'd properly woken up. The alien was sitting up in her pod, supported by some of those intelligent pillows that moved into the perfect ergonomic position. She was pale and her eyes were half-lidded, but after decades of being in a coma, she was allowed to look less than perfect.

"Beth, meet Ayla," Jenny introduced us. "She's Vhom's mother."

I took Ayla's hand in mine, as I'd done when she'd first started waking up. "It's a pleasure to finally be able to talk to you."

"I'm so confused," Ayla said, her voice hoarse from disuse.

Jenny held a high-tech straw to the woman's mouth and she took a sip, giving Jenny a grateful look. It seemed all of us humans were involved in caring for the Albyan females now. June stood next to a pod on the other side of the room, her back turned to me. The woman she was looking after seemed to be well enough to have a conversation.

What a change from only yesterday. And this was only the beginning. From experience, I knew that it would take these women a long time to get back to normal life. Even if Albyan technology could get their bodies back to their full strength faster than nature could on its own, their minds had been trapped for years. Nobody knew what effect that would have in the long run.

"I understand," I told Ayla when she'd stopped drinking. "I was in your situation once. I wasn't in a coma for as long as you, but I assume waking up from it is pretty much the same, no matter how long you were unconscious. It was very disorienting. It took me days to be able to differentiate between dreams and reality. Sometimes, I would see people in my room who weren't really there. Remnants of the dream world I'd lived in."

Jenny reached out and put a hand on my shoulder. "I didn't know."

I shrugged. "It's not like I talk about it a lot. It's in the past." I sighed and realised I was running my hand over the puckered scars along my neck. "Until today, I kept asking the universe: why me? Why did I have to be in that accident? Why did my husband have to die in it? Why did it have to leave me disfigured? But now, I can see how I'm the only one in this building who knows what these women are going through. What you, Ayla, will have to deal with in the coming weeks. I'm not sure I believe in fate, but if I did, being here among you now would seem like it was destiny."

"The stars brought you here," Ayla said weakly. "When you woke up, were you afraid to go back to sleep? Because I am."

I nodded. "Yes, sometimes. Other times, I wanted to go back into that dreamland and stay there forever. It seemed easier than facing reality. But it's different for you. You all have mates, families waiting for you. They will help you ease back into normal life."

"My mate," Ayla whispered. "Mate."

Her eyelids fluttered close, even though it was clear she was fighting her tiredness.

I squeezed her hand. "Don't worry. You'll just have a quick nap and then you'll wake up again. By then, your mate might be here."

"Mate," she whispered again before slipping into a deep sleep.

I exchanged a look with Jenny.

"Are you sure they're all going to stay awake?" she asked.

"I have no idea. I'm not a scientist nor a doctor. But now that our presence has caused them all to wake, I don't see how the Sleep could return. I'm sure Cyle will find answers. He has to."

13

Beth

He woke me in the middle of the night two days later. It felt like early morning, too early, but it could have been the middle of the day. I'd given up trying to keep to a normal rhythm and now slept when I got too tired. It had been nothing but chaos. Everyone looked for me for answers. In return, I waited for Cyle to get them. I trusted him to discover what was going on, but until then, I'd kept busy caring for the Albyan females, reassuring them, sharing my own experiences of what it had been like to wake from a coma.

"Beth, wake up."

He gently shook my shoulders until I blinked open my eyes.

"What? Is something wrong?" My words were slurred with tiredness.

"I found it!"

Pride, excitement and awe mixed in his hushed voice. He sounded like he wanted to shout it all out and only his consideration for my sleepiness stopped him from doing so.

"Found..."

"The cure!"

I sat up straight, all tiredness forgotten. "What?"

"The cure. I know how to heal the rest of the females. I've done it, Beth. I've finally done it."

"Show me."

He lifted me off the bed and carried me to the holobase. It was still activated, showing a globe full of glowing data that meant nothing to me.

"Here," Cyle said and pointed at a graph. He looked at me expectantly.

I hated to stifle his enthusiasm. "I'm sorry, but I have no idea what I'm looking at. You'll have to put it into simple terms for me. Remember, you're the genius, not me."

"You're the most brilliant female in the universe," he muttered lovingly and stroked my cheek. "My perfect match."

He turned off the holobase. "Let's try this another way. Albyans are programmed to have mates. There is one particular marker in our genome that determines who we're mated to. We found the same marker in Peritans - humans - plus an additional one. That's why I wrongly matched you to Obi. The first marker matched his, but not the second. Does that make sense so far?"

I nodded. "The second matched me to you."

Cyle grinned. "Yes. And the first, although that wasn't as clear a match, which is why the algorithms didn't show it during the first matching process. I'm now convinced that the second marker is more important for Albyan-Peritan matches than the first. Anyway, I had a look at some Albyan samples from several generations back and guess what I found?"

"The second marker?"

"Exactly. It's slightly different from what I found in your Peritan genome, but it's there. In the sleeping females, however, it's changed. At least it was, until you arrived on the planet."

"Are you saying our arrival changed their DNA?"

"In very simple terms, yes. It activated switches that were already there, putting changes into motion that I didn't understand or even see until now."

He smiled. I'd never seen him this relaxed before. A massive weight had been lifted from him. He could finally be free.

"But how did your father cause the Sleep?"

"Let me think of how to put this simply. The second marker has been naturally decaying over generations. Nobody realised because we always looked at the first marker when confirming matches. And not many Albyans wanted to have their mates found that way. They preferred the traditional route of letting themselves be led to their mate through their antennae's directions. My father had seen a decrease in fertility over the years. It's what he was researching. Now, I think that it has to do with the second marker decaying, but I need to do more research. By trying to cure the fertility issue, he inadvertently caused the Sleep."

Cyle took a deep breath. This wasn't an easy topic for him to talk about, so I waited patiently, giving him the time he needed.

"He created a bìoras that was supposed to fix the second marker."

"A what?" I asked.

"It's hard to explain. A kind of virus that spreads via pheromones. They're incredibly hard to detect until you know exactly what you're looking for."

"But you knew what you were looking for."

"Not at first," he admitted. "I couldn't explain how the females reacted to your presence - when I say *your*, I mean all of you Peritans, especially Jenny since she was the first. The pods our females were kept in were supposed to keep out any viruses. But they weren't designed to prevent bìoras from reaching the females."

"Wait. Are you saying we're all carrying these... bi-whatever and infected the women by accident?"

"Yes. It's not harmful to you and I doubt Peritan medicine would even know where to look for it. There might be some evolutionary reason for you carrying that bìoras. All this time, I was looking for two separate solutions to the Sleep: a cure and finding compatible females on our planets. I wouldn't have thought the two were one and the same."

I wanted to kiss him. His enthusiasm was sexy.

"So, in a nutshell, your father broke something in your females and we brought the stuff to fix it," I mused. "Is that right?"

Cyle chuckled. "In a very, very, very simplistic form. Yes. I will have to write that down; it's how I can explain it to the Council of Elders and everyone else.

They don't like it when I get too deep into the scientific context."

I reached up and stroked his cheek. He'd grown all stubbly in the past few days. Maybe I should ask him to let the scruff grow into a beard. It would look good on him.

"I love it when you talk sciency to me," I whispered. My thumb touched his bottom lip and before I knew what was happening, he'd sucked it into his mouth. He swirled his tongue around my thumb, sucking on it as if it was some tasty morsel. His eyes locked with mine. A pleasant shiver ran down my back and I felt my nipples pebble. This man affected me like no one ever before. He was sucking on my thumb, for goodness sake. That shouldn't make me all wet and needy. But it did.

"You found the cure," I said hoarsely. "That means your vow is fulfilled. I think it's time to celebrate."

He took my hand and gently pulled it back. It popped when he released my thumb from his lips.

"It will take time to synthesise the bioras into a drug that we can give to females across Albya, but yes. I agree with you. I want to finally make you my mate. If you will still have me."

"Have you?" I laughed. "I want nothing more."

He leaned down and pressed a hot kiss on my forehead.

"Then I will make you mine. But not here. Let me bring you home."

It had been over two weeks since I'd first met Cyle. And in all that time, I'd never seen his house. Our home. We'd live here together from now on. It was hard to believe. Ever since I'd arrived on Albya, I'd felt like a visitor. I'd stayed at a hotel, slept in a shuttle, then on a bed in Cyle's lab. He'd offered me to sleep at his house, but with him refusing to leave the lab building, it had seemed wrong.

I wasn't his mate yet. Not really. We'd not taken the final step.

But now we were about to.

Cyle lived - no, *we* lived at the edge of Priomh in a green, spacious part of the city. It felt more like a village than a capital city. The houses were mostly round glass domes, nothing like homes back on Earth. They almost looked like greenhouses if you ignored that they were perfectly circular, had windows, screens, colourful foggy walls and so on.

The shuttle landed on a paved circle surrounded by trees. The morning sun was just about reaching over the horizon, painting the glass of his home a pale orange. I couldn't see a street or other houses from here. We were completely enclosed by nature. I loved it.

"My brother's mate told me about a Peritan tradition," Cyle said and scooped me into his arms. "I shall carry you through the door. It's for good luck, right?"

I grinned and snuggled against his broad chest. "It is. But I bet you'd also try to carry me even without an Earth tradition."

Cyle laughed. "You know me so well already, leannan."

"What does that mean?"

"I will tell you later. When you're naked in front of me, ready to be worshipped."

Yet again, his words made me tremble. I twisted in his grip so I could put my hands on his naked chest.

"I can feel your heartbeat," I muttered, more to myself than to him.

"It beats for you. Only you."

He was such a romantic and I bet he didn't even know it.

Cyle carried me to the entrance of the large house. It was so strange to have a house without a roof, just seamless glass. I supposed rain would simply pearl down the surface, making it ideal for a planet that had very Scottish weather indeed. Not that I'd seen much of it, having been cooped up inside for weeks.

The double doors slid open soundlessly when we approached. "I'm going to programme everything to respond to you," Cyle promised. "After I've shown you the bedroom."

He winked at me.

"Yes, I think you should show me the bedroom right away. The rest of the tour can wait."

He hurried inside, pressing me tight against his chest. I didn't register the rooms we passed. I was way too occupied trying not to lick Cyle. My hormones were on overdrive. I wanted to touch him all over, lick him, kiss him, taste him. But I had enough self-control to keep my hands - and my tongue - to myself.

But all bets were off when we reached the bedroom, a massive circular room with a round bed in the centre. It had bright blue sheets that looked like silk. Shelves were built into the round walls and I assumed a wardrobe or other storage would be in the walls as well, but I didn't care. It was finally time to claim my mate.

14

Cyle

I sat her down on the bed. I didn't want to let go of her, but it would be easier to rip off her clothes while she wasn't in my arms.

There was no way I would be able to undress her slowly. I'd been waiting for too long. I knew that it was my fault, but that didn't make it any easier. My cock was aching to be pushed into her depths. My antennae tingled like crazy.

When I reached for the hem of her shirt, she grasped my wrists to stop me.

"Wait. My turn first. You've teased me for long enough."

"Teased you?" I asked breathlessly.

"Your kilt. It's time to find out what's under it."

I groaned. I supposed I had teased her. It had become a joke among the males mated to Peritan females. None of us had anticipated how intriguing they'd find our kilts. In retrospect, it made sense. They didn't know about our anatomy. I'd studied Peritans before we'd landed on their planet and I knew exactly what Beth was hiding under clothes. I knew her pussy was perfectly shaped to take my cock. But she didn't have that knowledge. Not yet.

I grinned and slowly lifted my kilt. My cock was curved upwards, rock hard and glistening with nectar. My petals trembled when cool air hit them.

"Wow," Beth muttered, her eyes wide. "The other girls mentioned flowers, but I thought they were kidding."

She put her hand around my shaft. I sucked in a sharp breath at the sensation. Her skin was so soft, so warm, her hand so tiny. She didn't quite manage to fully wrap her fingers around me. The rings at the base of my cock became tight, ready to push my nectar up the shaft and into my mate.

Not yet. I had to stay in control, no matter how much I wanted to throw her onto her back and claim her.

"What do you call them?" Beth asked, gently running a finger over one of my petals.

"Petals," I grunted. "And if you keep doing that, I won't last very long."

Beth smiled innocently before licking across my petals. My cock jerked in her hand.

"Stop it," I pleaded, but she was already taking me into her mouth. Her warm wetness enveloped me and I couldn't help but close my eyes. It was the best thing I'd ever felt in my life.

Her tongue swirled over my petals and they shivered in response. The rings around the shaft were vibrating, something they'd never done before. I knew they would do that, of course, but I'd expected it to happen once I was embedded within her pussy so they could stimulate her clit.

I was completely out of control. All that mattered were her lips moving along my cock, her tongue playing with my petals, her hand cupping my balls. She was driving me crazy.

"Beth," I groaned. "Mate."

She stopped just long enough to whisper, "Again. Say my name."

"Beth." My voice was hoarse with arousal. My heart was beating fast and my breath quickening. It felt like I was doing a strenuous workout instead of just standing her, having Beth do all the work. Her deft fingers massaged the base of my cock, caressing my balls, while her tongue did its magic around my petals. They seemed to fascinate her. She tried to suck at one, but that made them close around the head, almost trapping her lips.

She chuckled. "Will they do what I think they'll do?"

I forced myself to open my eyes and look down at her. My nectar coated her lips and chin. I wanted to bend down and lick her clean.

"They'll expand when I spill my seed in you," I explained. I was so breathless I had to stop and take a deep breath. "They'll lock us together. It's intended to make sure that my sperm can reach your eggs, fertilising you, but I believe you were given an injection on the Starlight?"

"Yes, contraception. Will it definitely work, considering we're different species?"

My heart fell a little. Did she not want offspring? She sounded worried about the potential of getting pregnant.

"I'm sure it works. Do you not want... I mean... I..."

"Children? One day. Yes, definitely. But not now." She looked up at me and smiled. "One day, I'd love to have a baby with you. Today, I just want to feel you inside me without having to worry about the consequences."

I sighed in relief. "I'm glad. Now stop touching my petals before I come. I want the first time to be inside of you."

Beth nodded. "Yes. Claim me. Make me your mate."

My antennae shivered in delight at hearing her words. She wanted me as much as I craved her.

This was the moment. But as much as I wanted to claim her this very moment, I remembered what I'd been taught. Prepare your female, show her how much you love her. It was time to worship her body like she'd worshipped my cock.

I took a few steadying breaths before I reached for her skirt. It had the same colourful pattern as her head wrap, yellows and reds intermingling.

"Hurry up," she muttered. "I want you."

I pulled down her skirt, exposing a tiny black undergarment hiding what I so desperately craved.

"I've been wearing pretty knickers for the past two weeks now, hoping it would come to this," she admitted. "I was running out of clean underwear. Tomorrow, you would have got bland cotton knickers."

"You're beautiful no matter what you wear. Besides, from now on, I think you shouldn't wear anything at all. It just gets in the way."

Beth giggled, a delightful sound that echoed through the room. "Like you under your kilt? I suppose it has its advantages."

"Yes," I growled. "I will be able to take you day in, day out. At the lab. In my office. In the relief room. Here. In the garden. In-"

"Stop talking," Beth commanded, already pulling her shirt over her head. Underneath, two triangles of fabric held her beautiful breasts. Peritans had larger breasts than Albyans and I couldn't have been happier about that fact.

"Why do you bind them such?" I asked.

"You mean my bra? These girls are heavy. I need the support. Besides, I don't want everyone to see my nipples poking out when you make me aroused. Which is basically all the time."

I made her aroused. My cock twitched at the thought. I'd been hard ever since I'd laid my eyes on her and had to make frequent trips to the relief room to get rid of the painful erection, but it pleased me to no ends that it had been similar for her.

I looked for a way to get the *bra* off her. She grinned when she saw my confusion and reached behind her.

"Men never know how to open these," she chuckled. "I guess that doesn't change, no matter what planet you're on."

She let the garment fall down, exposing her full breasts. Her dark nipples stood within a circle of pebbled skin as if to guide me to the centre.

"You're beautiful," I whispered. I barely dared to touch her. She was a goddess and I a mere mortal. I wasn't worthy.

"So are you."

She shot a look at my cock. "I've never seen a more gorgeous dick. It's like a work of art."

She tried to reach for me again, but I captured her hands. "Lie on your back. It's time for me to return the pleasure you've already given me."

"As much as I love foreplay, I need you inside me." Her voice was barely a whisper. Her pupils were dilated, her lips parted. She was ripe and ready to be claimed.

"Then I will keep foreplay for the next time. Are you ready for me even without preparation?"

Beth laughed. "I've been ready for you ever since I met you."

She shimmied out of her undergarments, then lay on her back and spread her legs for me. Drops of wetness glistened like diamonds. Her pussy was swollen with need. I couldn't resist the temptation. I dipped a finger into her, eliciting a soft moan. She was warm and tight and trembling with anticipation. My mate ached to be claimed, it was clear to see.

I licked my finger, tasting her nectar. Sweet like honey. As much as I wanted to lick her pussy, taste more of her, drink her juices, I knew I wouldn't last much longer. Even just seeing her spread out for me made me close to coming. I'd never thought a female could have this effect on me.

"Claim me," she said, looking straight into my eyes. "Take me, mate."

I needed no second invitation. I aligned myself with her opening while taking her thighs in my hands, holding her in place. I took one last look at her, then pushed inside, past that tight band of resistance, until I was fully embedded. She was tight but not painfully so. She was made for me. The stars had created us as perfect mates and our bodies were attuned to each other. I was the key in her lock, shaped exactly the way I had to be to fit.

My petals started vibrating. They were no longer under my control. I knew that I wouldn't be able to close them once they'd opened, locking us together. But first, I would fuck her like we both craved.

I gave her another moment to adjust, then I pulled out almost entirely. Her inner muscles grabbed my cock as if they wanted to prevent me from leaving. I grinned. I'd never leave. She was mine.

Beth moaned loudly when I pushed in again, so deep that my balls pushed against her mound.

"Yes, that's the spot. Hit it again."

I set a slow pace, moving in rhythm with the vibrations of my petals. The rings around my shaft started quavering, too, eliciting yet more moans from Beth. My cock was made to pleasure her. It pleased me immensely to see her quiver beneath me, her hands grabbing her breasts as if trying to hold on to them for support. Her head was thrown back, her throat exposed. I licked my lips, resisting the urge to kiss her. Later.

I was close, but I needed her to come at the same time as me. I reached between us, finding the delicate nub I'd read about, and gently drew circles around it.

Beth gasped, her eyes flying open. "Harder!"

I gave it to her. I let go of all restraint and fucked her with every ounce of strength I possessed. I rammed into her depths, her moans encouraging me, teasing me, while my petals quaked ever faster.

I knew the instant she was about to come. I felt it, even though I didn't know how. I arched my back and pushed in deeper than I had before. My seed erupted from between the petals and I roared my release. Her inner muscles milked me as she shattered into a row of desperate screams.

Stars exploded before my eyes and my vision swam for a moment. I dimly felt my petals expand, pressing against her insides, locking us together. Their vibrations didn't subside while the rings around my base spurred Beth on further. She writhed on the bed, her limbs shaking uncontrollably.

I lowered myself onto her, making sure I kept my weight on my knees and elbows so I didn't crush her. I captured her mouth in mine, swallowing her moans as she came again and again. Only when my petals stopped moving did she finally still. She was breathing hard but kept kissing me, her lips seeking mine whenever I pulled away to tease her. With my lower hands, I started caressing her breasts, finally getting to feel her hard nipples. She arched her back when I twirled them between my fingers.

"It feels incredible," she muttered. "I feel so full."

"Best feeling in the universe," I agreed before taking one of her nipples into my mouth. I lazily suckled on it while I basked in the afterglow. My hot seed was pooling around my petals and I imagined what it would be like to have it sire new life. Would it feel the same as now when I bred my mate?

"Don't stop." Beth held my head in place, her fingers curling around my hair. Amused, I continued to lap at her breast. I'd promised her to worship her body. This was only the beginning. I was going to explore every part of her. I'd claimed her, but I'd never stop worshipping her.

15

Beth

I woke in his arms, safe and warm. I dimly remembered that he'd pulled out of me while I'd been half-asleep, cleaned me with a wet cloth before wrapping us in a blanket. Not that I needed one. He was hot enough. In more ways than one.

I ached a little but it was a pleasant reminder of what had happened. He'd claimed me. We were now officially mates. Well, we still had to do the handfasting ceremony, but in my mind, we were a proper couple. I'd never believed that marriage was necessary for two people to confess their love.

Yes. I loved him. With all my heart. One part of my heart would always beat for my husband and I'd never forget him, but I was moving on and it felt good. A new life.

Yesterday had been the first time I'd undressed without paying any attention to my scars. I reached up and realised my head wrap was gone. Probably somewhere on the floor. But it didn't matter. I didn't care if Cyle saw my scarred head. I knew he loved me no matter what I looked like. I had felt it, his love, when he'd held me in his arms, his cock buried inside me. It had been incredible. The combination of his vibrating petals and rings, the pounding of his cock, his feral grunts as he'd come, it had all made this the best sex I'd ever had. I had no idea I was even capable of coming as often as I'd had. Crazy. Now I knew why the other human women spent so much time with their mates. They'd all been happy to spend time at the lab to help the Albyan females, but their mates were never far away, always hovering nearby. I bet quite a few of them had done the deed in the toilets, or relief room, as they called it.

I didn't want to leave this bed ever again. Having Cyle's arms around me made me feel protected. I'd been on the move for so long, never stopping in fear of the past catching up with me, that simply being here in this room with him was special. I wished I could stop all clocks on the planet. I didn't want to go back to reality. If only Cyle wasn't so important. Why couldn't he be some lowly peasant who nobody would miss if he spent a week in bed with his new mate?

But Cyle was the First Scientist of my new home planet. He didn't have the freedom I wanted us to have.

We'd always have more duties than the average couple, but we'd get through it together. As mates.

"You're awake," he muttered sleepily.

"And so are you."

Cyle groaned. "I think we overslept."

"Was there a time we had to get up?"

"No, I suppose not. I'm not used to staying in bed this long."

Yes, because he was a workaholic who needed to be taught to take care of himself, not just of everyone else.

"Let's have breakfast," I suggested. "Here, together. I want this moment to last a little longer before we go back into the real world."

He kissed the back of my neck. His hot breath made my skin tingle. Maybe we should skip breakfast and have some more bedroom fun instead.

"Jenny and Thorrn have started a strange new tradition that they call 'breakfast in bed'," he said, deadly serious. "Maybe we should try that also."

I chuckled. "Have you never had breakfast in bed? Never, ever?"

"Why would I do that? It's unhygienic. Besides, the food processor isn't in the bedroom. It makes no sense.

But Thorrn says it's great fun, so I think we should try it."

"Alright, let's try this *new* tradition." I had to stop myself from laughing. Sometimes it was easy to forget that we came from very different cultures.

Four arms came in very handy when cooking. To be fair, most of what Cyle was doing involved telling a machine what to cook for us, but he was able to juggle way more dishes at the same time than I could. I'd followed him into the kitchen - which was really a large dining room with a tiny area on one side that held the food processor and a sink-like basin - to see more of the house. I'd get him to teach me how to use all the technology in this place later. For now, I quite enjoyed being served breakfast.

Back on the bed, I wrapped the blanket around me like a dress. I had no problem being naked in Cyle's company, but it felt weird to eat without clothes on. Cyle gave me a strange look but didn't say anything.

"I guess we better transport my stuff here soon," I said while he was spreading plates and bowls around the centre of the round bed. "Or I'll have to start wearing your clothes."

Cyle chortled. "Or we could simply use the fabricator. It can make whatever garments you desire."

"Anything? Even an elf dress with long flowy sleeves?"

"I have no idea what you're talking about, but yes. I will show you. As long as you can give the fabricator all the specifications it needs, it can produce whatever you want."

"That's amazing. It's like online shopping but with instant delivery and for free."

He laughed again. "Not quite free. We have to pay for the base material cubes it uses, but don't worry about money. I earn way more than I could ever spend. Plus, you get a stipend as a Peritan mate."

Back on the Starlight, they'd taught us about the currencies used on Albya, but I hadn't actually had to use money yet.

"Do you even have shops?" I asked. "Or do you get everything from your fabricator?"

"We have shops, of course. There is a renewed focus on handcrafted objects. Back to basics, back to our roots. When the Sleep happened, many people blamed technology. We'd gone too far, they said, manipulating our own bodies and pretending to be deities. I wonder how things will change now that we have a cure for the Sleep."

His eyes widened slightly. "I can't believe I just said that. A cure. It doesn't feel real yet."

I put a hand on his. "I'm so proud of you."

He held my hand to his lips and pressed a row of gentle kisses along my knuckles. "It would never have happened without you. You're the key to the cure." Cyle smiled. "And the key to my heart."

Another set of kisses. I wanted to swoon. He was such a romantic.

We seemed to remember the food between us at the same time. He let go of my hand and started piling various interesting looking dishes into a large wooden bowl. When he'd added a bit of everything, he gave me the bowl along with an intricately carved spork. This wasn't just a simple utensil, it was a piece of art. Probably an heirloom.

"I wasn't sure what you'd like so I made all my favourites," Cyle explained while filling his own bowl. "Try that moutoo nut puree. As a child, I always told my mother that I could subsist on nothing else. It always makes me think of her."

His antennae quivered with emotion.

I took a sporkful of the pale yellow puree. It tasted like roasted hazelnuts mixed with maple juice. Delicious, although I couldn't imagine it as a main meal. But then, as a child, I would have happily lived on nothing but red velvet cupcakes.

"I like it," I said when I realised he was waiting for a reaction. "It would make a great dessert."

His eyes twinkled with mirth. "I guess that means I only need to leave you a tiny portion and can eat the rest." He pointed at the nut puree bowl which was still almost full. "All mine."

I laughed. "Knock yourself out."

His smile disappeared. "You want me to harm myself? Wait, that's one of your strange Peritan idioms. Am I right?"

"You are indeed. Well spotted."

A proud grin spread across his face. "I'm getting better at it. Thorrn gets confused way more often than me."

"That's why you're the scientist and not him. Now, what is this green stuff over here?"

It looked like mushy peas with tiny pieces of something crimson.

Dish by dish, I worked myself through Cyle's favourites. Most of them were sweet things, giving me an idea of what a sweet tooth he really had. I was glad when I discovered that kylam stalks were salty, reminding me a bit of asparagus but as if it had been pickled in vinegar.

I only managed to eat half my bowl until I was full. Incredulously, Cyle didn't just empty his bowl in record time, he also had second helpings. When he finally put down his spork, all the moutoo nut puree was gone.

"This eating in bed will become our tradition now, too," he decreed. "We will do this as often as we can."

I wanted to squeeze him. He was so adorable. My adorable alien.

At the lab, everyone gave us knowing glances and happy smiles.

"Finally," Jenny snickered when she spotted us. "It's taken you long enough."

"How are the females?" Cyle asked, ignoring everyone's looks.

Vhom hurried towards us. "Awake, all of them," he gleamed. "My mother has taken her first steps. We're treating everyone with muscle stimulators to help their bodies recover as quickly as possible."

"Excellent. I need to do something in my lab, but I will do a building-wide broadcast as soon as I'm done."

Cyle bent down, whispering so only I could hear. "I will try and synthesize the bìoras. It shouldn't take long, if all my calculations are correct. Then I can send the formula to the other research centres across Albya to create enough of the bìoras to cure all our females."

I could see him already working on his next steps in his mind. His gaze was becoming absent and I knew he'd be in full scientist mode as soon as he got into his office.

"Do you need me?" I asked.

"Need you? Always. Need you for this particular task? No." He lifted me into his arms and kissed me. Around us, people whooped, but I didn't care. We kissed as if there was nobody else. As if we had all the time in the world. As if he wasn't carrying the responsibility for an entire planet on his shoulders.

When we finally broke apart, he sat me down on the floor but kept his hands around my waist.

"Don't go far. I can't think when I'm not near you. My antennae itch and that's distracting."

"I can recommend a salve for that," Thorrn hollered. "Although there's a much better cure."

He and some of the other males roared with laughter.

Cyle waved them off. "There's only one cure I'm interested just now."

He hurried away. He definitely wouldn't leave his lab until he had that pheromone virus synthesised. If he took too long, I'd make sure he got some rest and food, but for now, I joined the other women.

I spent the morning talking to several Albyan women. Most of them were well enough to sit up and two were already walking about, but one elderly woman was still in her pod, looking very pale. She'd introduced herself as Mo'na, but since speaking exhausted her, she'd not said much since. It was clear though that she didn't want to go back to sleep, so I sat by her side, telling her stories just like I'd had when the women had still all been asleep.

"...And they all lived happily ever after," I ended my tale.

Mo'na smiled and patted my hand. "Thank you. I pray the Lady Beyra will grant you a happy life as well." She touched her thumb to her index finger in prayer. "I heard you in my dreams. I am grateful."

It took her a moment before she was strong enough to continue.

"I want to give you something. For gratitude. My son will give it to you."

"You don't need to give me anything," I protested, but she took my hand and made me shut up with a single look. She'd once been a strong woman and I was sure that she would be again as soon as she recovered.

"Your mate is from my clan," she wheezed. "It's an honour to welcome you to our family."

My eyes burned. Don't cry. Not now.

"Thank you," was all I could say before my voice caught in my throat.

I waited until Mo'na had fallen asleep before leaving the room. It was time to check on Cyle. Before I reached his office, an Albyan stopped me. He was older than my mate and seemed strangely familiar.

"I'm Bayl of Clan Lannadh. I have something for you," he said, the words tumbling from his mouth. "My mother told me to give it to you. It's our family's handfasting cloth. I was never able to have a mate, so it's been gathering dust all this time. I agree with her that you're the best person to have it."

He reverently handed me a folded piece of green tartan cloth.

"Thank you," I whispered. This time, I couldn't stop a tear running down my cheek. He and his mother were strangers, yet they were ready to give me something so precious. "I can't accept that. It belongs to you."

Bayl smiled. "If I ever find a mate, you can return it to me. I never thought I would, but now I have new hope. Maybe one day, you and your mate can be at my handfasting."

I bowed my head. "It would be an honour."

I held the cloth to my chest and hurried away before I could cry even more. I burst into Cyle's office without knocking. He was bent over the holobase, deep in thought, but looked up when I entered.

He was by my side in two strides. "What's wrong? Why are you crying?"

I gave him a weak smile, fighting yet more tears. "Cyle. Would you like to do the handfasting ceremony with me?"

I held up the cloth and his eyes widened.

"I would like nothing more, my mate." He swept me into his arms and kissed away my tears.

EPILOGUE

One month later

Beth

The standing stones towered above us like silent sentinels. They were much larger than any standing stones I'd been to back home in Scotland. They would be witnesses to our handfasting ceremony; the first that had taken place in this sacred location in a generation. Half the planet seemed to be here. I didn't recognise most of the Albyans, but I felt honoured that all these strangers had come all this way to celebrate with us. Our feast earlier had been just for close friends and family, but there were refreshment stations set up all around the stones for guests to help themselves. I'd barely been able to eat anything, but Cyle had managed to feed me a few bites of my favourite Albyan dishes.

I would have preferred a quiet ceremony, just the two of us, but Cyle had let himself be persuaded that our handfasting would be a symbol to all of Albya, a clear sign that we were entering a new era. The Sleep had been cured. Not a single Albyan woman was still trapped in a coma. Most had been reunited with their mates and were back home, although some still needed medical attention. Cyle had calculated that only about a quarter of the population was female now, but today, that ratio was very different. All the other human women had come, along with many of the Albyans I'd looked after when they'd first awoken. The next batch of humans would arrive tomorrow, but by then, Cyle and I would be on our honeymoon.

"I didn't think so many would come," Cyle muttered under his breath. "Look, the entire Council of Elders is here. And the male in the purple kilt over there is my old mentor."

"How about we have our mating ceremony in private?"

He nodded. "Most definitely."

Albyan tradition dictated that today, we would promise to be with each other for one year and one day. A sort of test phase. Then, if we still wanted to be together, we'd have the mating ceremony next year. It felt like something Cyle had come up, even though I knew it was an ancient tradition.

One of the elders waved us over. He was the same guy who'd done the ceremony for Thorrn and Jenny. "Are you ready?"

I exchanged a look with Cyle and nodded. My stomach was full of drunken butterflies that kept bumping into each other. I couldn't wait to have it over with so I could spend some alone time with Cyle.

"Do you have your cloth?" the elder asked. Hav? Havn? Havm? How embarrassing that I couldn't remember his name even though he was about to almost-marry us.

I handed it to him. The green tartan fabric was faded at the edges. I had no idea how old it was, but I bet it had been in Mo'na's family for generations.

"Excellent. Cyle, you will enter the circle from between the tallest two stones. Beth, you will enter from over here. I will be waiting in the centre."

He pulled out an intricately carved horn and held it to his lips. At the surprisingly deep sound, silence fell and the gathered guests moved out of the stone circle.

I smoothed my dress. I'd made it myself using the fabricator and it fit perfectly. The main skirt ended at my knees, but a lace overlay continued to my feet, touching the grass. The neckline was wider than what I was used to, but I wanted the necklace Cyle had given me on full display. The green gem perfectly matched his eyes. Every time I looked at it, I felt like I was gazing into his loving eyes. It made me all warm and fuzzy. And with him spending a lot of time in his lab and me now officially working at the same institute to help with rehabilitation, I didn't get to see him as often as I wanted. It's why our honeymoon was going to be special. Nothing but spending lots and lots of time with Cyle.

I waited until Cyle had taken his position at the opposite end of the stone circle. The elder now stood in the very centre where the grass had been pressed into a Celtic knot. He blew his horn again. As if in a dream, I slowly walked towards him. It didn't feel real. My feet seemed to float rather than hit solid ground. The silence was ethereal, only broken by slow, deep blows of the horn. My dress swept across the grass, the hem getting heavy with dew.

I felt everyone watching me. I didn't take my eyes off Cyle who was matching his steps to my rhythm, but I knew that every eye was on us. I already mentally prepared myself for what would happen if I stumbled.

One foot in front of the other.

By the time we both reached the elder, I was a trembling mess.

He spread the cloth over his arms, presenting it to us.

"Have you, Bethany Jones, freely agreed to become the loving mate of Cyle of Clan Lannadh?"

"I have," I said as loud as I could.

"Have you, Cyle of Clan Lannadh, freely agreed to become the loving mate of Bethany Jones?"

Cyle looked at me, his eyes sparkling. "Aye, I have."

My heart threatened to jump from my chest. I wanted to kiss him right now, but the ceremony wasn't over yet.

"Please hold out your hands," Havn said.

We did. Each of my wrists was framed by two of Cyle. I linked my pinkie fingers with his.

Havn raised the cloth to the sky for everyone to see. "Upon this day, you will join as mates. For one rotation and one day, your lives will be entwined."

He lay the fabric across our arms and smoothened it.

"Upon this day, your souls will form an unbreakable knot."

The elder took the ends of the strip of cloth and wrapped them once around our hands. I locked eyes with Cyle and only felt how the elder added a second layer.

"Upon this day, your bond will be as strong as this ribbon. You are now tied together, two beings as one, until you choose to renew your vows at the Stones of our ancestors or choose to walk separate ways."

The fabric tightened as the elder twisted it into a knot at the top of our hands. Beneath the cloth, Cyle took my hands between his. The love reflecting in his eyes was all I needed. The words the elder spoke were pretty, but what mattered was what we both felt in our hearts.

"From this day on, you are lawful mates. Bethany and Cyle of Clan Lannadh, I present you to your clan and all clans of Albya."

Cheers drifted towards us, clapping and the sound of drums, but I didn't take my eyes off Cyle. We communicated without words, declaring our love.

"You can kiss her now," the elder whispered to Cyle.

My mate smirked. "I know."

He pulled one of his hands from the knot and cupped my cheek.

"My leannan. My love."

And then he kissed me, sealing the bond, making me the happiest woman in the universe.

The stars had led us to each other. It hadn't been an easy journey, but now we were where we'd always meant to be.

The sacred stones stood guard as we celebrated our union, one of many to come.

Albya was going to survive. And we'd be part of this new world.

THE END

If you've not read the other two books in the series yet, start with Thorrn.

For more alien romance set in the same world, check out The Intergalactic Guide to Humans, *a series involving everything from probing and space pirates to adorable alien bunnies.*

Would you like your own Albyan Highlander? Join the Hot Tatties Dating Agency: skyemackinnon.com/hottatties

Want to know what he's hiding under that kilt?
Go to my website to find out!
(*definitely not safe for work*)

skyemackinnon.com/starlightnsfw

ABOUT THE AUTHOR

Skye MacKinnon is a USA Today & International Bestselling Author whose books are filled with strong heroines who don't have to choose.

She embraces her Scottishness with fantastical Scottish settings and a dash of mythology, no matter if she's writing about Celtic gods, aliens, cat shifters, or the streets of Edinburgh.

When she's not typing away at her favourite cafe, Skye loves dried mango, as much exotic tea as she can squeeze into her cupboards, and being covered in pet hair by her tiny demonic cat.

Subscribe to her newsletter:
skyemackinnon.com/newsletter

facebook.com/skyemackinnonauthor
twitter.com/skye_mackinnon
instagram.com/skyemackinnonauthor
bookbub.com/authors/skye-mackinnon
goodreads.com/SkyeMacKinnon

9 781913 556457